BOUNTY HUNTER'S MOON

A Shawn Starbuck Western

Ray Hogan

Thorndike Press • Chivers Press
Thorndike, Maine USA   Bath, England

This Large Print edition is published by Thorndike Press, USA and by Chivers Press, England.

Published in 2000 in the U.S. by arrangement with Golden West Literary Agency.

Published in 2000 in the U.K. by arrangement with Golden West Literary Agency.

U.S. Hardcover 0-7862-2421-5 (Western Series Edition)
U.K. Hardcover 0-7540-4097-6 (Chivers Large Print)
U.K. Softcover 0-7540-4098-4 (Camden Large Print)

The text of this Large Print edition is unabridged.
Other aspects of the book may vary from the original edition.

Set in 16 pt. Plantin by Rick Gundberg.

Printed in the United States on permanent paper.

British Library Cataloguing in Publication Data available

Library of Congress Cataloging-in-Publication Data

Hogan, Ray, 1908–
Bounty hunter's moon : a Shawn Starbuck western / by Ray Hogan.
p. cm.
ISBN 0-7862-2421-5 (lg. print : hc : alk. paper)
1. Starbuck, Shawn (Fictitious character) — Fiction.
2. Frontier and pioneer life — New Mexico — Fiction.
3. New Mexico — Fiction. 4. Large type books. I. Title.
PS3558.O3473 B67 2000
813′.54—dc21 99-089090

BOUNTY HUNTER'S MOON

1

"Dead!" Starbuck echoed heavily. "My brother — dead?"

Jess, the balding, round-faced owner of the Mesilla saloon where Shawn had halted for a drink on his way through, nodded, mopping at the countertop.

"Was what Augie said — leastwise, that's how he savvied it."

"Augie?"

"Stagecoach driver. Goes through here on the run east. Said he'd been told to pass the word along at his stops. Reckon you must've, some time or other, made the arrangements."

Starbuck picked up his glass of rye whiskey and downed it in a single gulp. *The end of the search,* he thought, but he answered the bartender's assumption.

"Yeh. I've been knocking about the country for years looking for Ben and asking folks to sort of watch out for him. Guess somebody remembered. That driver have anything else to say?"

"Said it was somebody by the name of

Bishop that was trying to reach you. Lawman, according to Augie — over in the Slaughter Valley side of the Territory. You know him?"

Arlie Bishop . . . Marshal Arlie Bishop of Tannekaw, a town near the Arizona border . . . Shawn glanced about the small saloon, deserted except for him and its owner at that early hour. Outside, in the tree-shaded plaza of the drowsy settlement, birds were making preparation for the spring that was already upon them.

"Go back about four years," he said. "Sort of helped him get started at his job."

Jess hung his damp mop-rag on a convenient nail behind the bar. "Appears he's the one knowing about your brother. Was you this Bishop's deputy?"

"Guess you could say that," Starbuck murmured.

He hadn't actually worn a star for Arlie Bishop — had merely acted, briefly, as his deputy. Bishop, fresh from the East with his wife, Carla, and a small daughter, had applied for the job as town marshal by mail after hearing of the settlement's need from a friend.

A stranger to the West, he had no real idea of what the job consisted, and had assumed it to be one paralleling the ordinary constable or village policeman's duties, with which he had a nodding acquaintance. He had been hired, moved himself and his family to the rough-edged cowtown of Tannekaw, and promptly discovered that he was well over his depth in trouble.

A lawman in a town such as Tannekaw bore little resemblance to the police officers with whom he was familiar; his job was not one of scolding school boys, bedding down local drunks, and serving legal papers, but one that called for facing up to hardcase gun-slingers, wild cowhands, and, in general, making a stand against the lawless element that sought continually to take over.

Bishop had just pinned on his star and was struggling to cope when Shawn had ridden into the settlement on his way to Mexico. It had become quickly apparent to him that Arlie Bishop, while eager and willing, would not be able to fulfill his obligations — would, in fact, probably lose his life in attempting to do so; but given time and experience, he should be capable of handling the job.

Starbuck had stepped in, sided the new lawman against the bullying aggressions of cowhands from a nearby ranch bent on avenging the death of their boss, and later substituted himself for the lawman in a showdown against the cattleman brother who came looking for vengeance also.

Eventually matters had worked out for

Arlie Bishop after that and Starbuck had ridden on. He'd heard no more from the lawman and his wife, Carla, who Shawn now recalled as being an extraordinarily beautiful woman having difficulty adjusting to western ways.

But Ben — his brother — dead . . . That would take some adjusting on his part. It was hard to accept. He'd always recognized the possibility of it happening, but that was making it no less difficult to believe.

"Augie, that driver, did he have any details — like where it happened, and how?"

The bartender poured a glass of liquor for himself, refilled Starbuck's. "Nope — leastwise he didn't mention none. Only said this Bishop was wanting to get word to you. Reckon he figures you'll look him up and find out firsthand what it's all about."

"What I'll do," Starbuck agreed. "Sure obliged to you, Jess."

The barman shrugged. "*Por nada.* Recollect you saying one time when you dropped by that it was family business keeping you on the move, hunting him. It still important?"

"Pa's estate," Starbuck said. "He died leaving a will saying that I had to find Ben and bring him back to meet with the lawyer before things could be settled."

"It a lot of money?"

The amount involved was in the neighborhood of thirty thousand dollars, but it was a brash question even coming from a friend and Starbuck ignored it.

"Been chasing Ben around the country for a lot of years — near seven, in fact. I think he's actually been sort of dodging me, figuring maybe I'm looking for him to take him back so's he can patch things up with Pa."

"You ain't never caught up with him in all that time?"

"Got close a few times, but not to where I could talk to him. Even tried leaving letters with lawmen here and there explaining why I wanted to see him, but I guess he never got them. I don't think he has much truck with lawmen."

Jess stared off through the open doorway of his establishment and wagged his head. "Been a tough shake for you — spending your life trailing him."

Starbuck's wide shoulders stirred. A tall, muscular man with slatelike, blue eyes and dark hair, there was a deep quiet to him — a remoteness instilled by the endless, disappointing trails, the wild violence of many towns, and the long, silent prairies over which he'd ridden — that set him apart and marked him as a man best left alone.

"Man has to play the cards dealt him," he said quietly, brushing at his full mustache.

"Reckon it's done with now — if what that stagecoach driver said is straight. Any chance he could've got things garbled?"

Again the barman shook his head. "Expect it'll be close to the facts. Old Augie ain't the smartest man that ever come down the pike, but like as not, he said what had been told him. Of course he got it maybe fifth or sixth hand so it could've been a mite stretched or mixed up. Was it me, I'd sort of bank on it. . . . You heading west for this here Tannekaw right away?"

"Sooner I talk to Arlie Bishop, the quicker I'll know what it's all about."

Jess studied Starbuck's set features for a long moment. Somewhere off along the outskirts of the town a cow lowed, mournfully protesting the tardy attention of a neglectful owner.

"Sounds like maybe you're misdoubting what you're hearing."

Shawn pulled off his hat and ran long fingers through his thick hair, curling down onto his neck and in need of a trimming.

"Somehow it's mighty hard to believe."

"Why? Plenty of men get shot up, or maybe throwed by a horse or run over by a herd of cattle every day. Could happen to him."

Shawn replaced his wide-brimmed hat. "I know that. Guess it being my brother we're talking about, I can't set it in my mind," he said, and pulling back from the counter, he extended his hand to the saloon man.

"I'll say again, Jess, I'm obliged to you. Expect I'd best be on my way."

The bartender nodded, took Starbuck's fingers into his own. "Already said — forget the thanks."

Shawn turned for the door and the hitch rack beyond where the big sorrel gelding he rode was waiting.

"I'll be dropping back by again one of these days. I'll take it as a favor if you'll thank that stagecoach driver — Augie — for me."

"Can figure it's done," Jess said, and added, "Good luck."

Starbuck nodded, and moving on through the open doorway, stepped out into the early morning sunlight.

2

Starbuck had wintered in the tail of Texas country, working cattle on a ranch south of Laredo for a time. When that job played out, he rode the border making inquiries as to Ben, known also as Damon Friend, and, as usual, turned up nothing that was of help.

He had not suffered from disappointment. Failure had long since become more the expected than the exception, and he had learned years ago to take it with no particular emotion and simply continue doggedly at his quest.

The search for his brother had been his life, and while that fact was called to his attention on occasion, as it had been in Mesilla by the saloon owner, he never dwelled upon it to any great extent. In truth, Shawn Starbuck knew little else but the search.

Leaving the family farm on the Muskingum River in Ohio after the death of his father, Hiram, he had been no more than a farm boy, inexperienced in all but the usual chores and accomplishments associated with that sort of life.

He had ridden directly into the raw frontier world of the West, and thanks to the rigid, hew-to-the-line type of upbringing that his father and his mother, Clare, had given him, he was able to hold his own, adapt, and become a part of the rugged world into which he had been thrust.

There had been no money to finance the quest for Ben, who had walked off the farm after a dispute with old Hiram over chores assigned but not fulfilled, and to pay his way Shawn had taken jobs whenever necessary, thus creating a system in which he learned to be expert in many things while working his way to and fro across the land.

He had reached the point where the thought of living a life of his own, realizing the dream of having a family, owning a ranch, raising cattle and prize horses, no longer occupied a corner of his mind. The fulfillment of Hiram Starbuck's proviso that he find Ben had eventually taken over wholly and unconsciously built for him a nomadic way of life that now was simply his nature.

Some looked upon him with real, but always carefully concealed, disdain; to them he was a drifter, a saddlebum, a man with no roots and therefore no future. They were judging him by their own standard of values; none took into consideration the freeness of spirit, the broad accumulation of knowledge, the familiarity with the vast land, and the countless towns and numberless people he became acquainted with.

Few, if any, ever learned to appreciate the indescribable peace of riding across a quiet, starlit prairie on a summer's night or heard the music of a gentle wind moving through towering pine trees that seemed to breach the clouds. Most never troubled to note the beauty of an eagle soaring effortlessly across the blue arch of the sky, or felt the exhilarating lash of a snow-burdened rain whipping in from the north on a fall day.

Men sought ease — warmth when it was cold, coolness when it was hot — and in so doing were lost to the natural gifts that were theirs for the taking. No man sitting in his leather rocker, satisfied with the comfort supplied by four walls and a roof, could know the pure excitement of a swollen mountain stream unexpectedly rushing down upon him, or the breathless moments of tension when a gun becomes the ultimate answer to a problem — but to Shawn Starbuck this was life itself, and it was doubtful he would, or could, abandon it now that the need to continue the search for his brother appeared to be over.

But at the close of this fifth day since riding out of Mesilla, as he halted in a small, dinty meadow high on a hill overlooking the valley in which the town of Tannekaw lay like an irregular shaped jewel glowing with yellow lamplight facets, he was giving the matter no thought. As was his custom, he would make such a decision when the moment to do so was upon him.

Darkness had closed in on the land, and the moon that had been increasing in size with each night's passage was not yet above the smoky hills to the east. It had been an easy journey, one he had made steadily but with no overt haste, and now as he looked down upon the distant settlement, he had a moment during which he felt a reluctance to continue, to learn for certain that Ben was dead.

For, to his thinking, it somehow meant failure on his part. He had set out at his father's bidding to find his brother, return him, theoretically, to the family — if only from a legal standpoint. Death had beat him to it. Perhaps, if he had tried harder, had covered more miles, ignored the delays that had often turned him aside when he had been close, he might have reached Ben, and, in so doing, circumvented the end.

But he had not — and there was never anything gained by thinking of what might have been; like a river rushing on to join the sea, there was no calling the past back. A man had no choice but to live with it.

Half turning, Starbuck threw his glance to the east. The moon was now breaking over the horizon, starting its climb and already spreading its glow over the hills and flats and the deep-shadowed canyons. He allowed his eyes to drift for a time, savoring the view; and then coming back around, he swung off his horse and, ground-reining the big sorrel, moved to the edge of the meadow. There, on his heels, he again fell into a study of the settlement, recalling what he could of the town and its people.

It had been four years, almost to the month, since he'd been there, Shawn realized, and the remembrance of Carla Bishop was still strong in his memory. He wondered if she had changed much, if she was still as beautiful as she had been then. Carla had stirred him deeply — a feeling that he discovered she shared — but she was another man's wife and that had written finish to any ideas that might have entered his mind.

It would be good to see her again and to renew his friendship with Arlie, too. Evidently Bishop had made a success of being a lawman else he would not still be there after so long a time. Shawn had thought as much; Bishop, while lacking some of the essentials in the beginning, was possessed by a driving determination to make something of himself and become a man of importance. The only question still to be answered would seem to be to what degree Arlie had realized his goals.

Rising, Starbuck swung his attention off to the west, to the lengthy flat studded with cedars, rabbitbush, and gaunt cholla cactus that flowed toward another range of mountains now only vague, mysterious shapes in the distance. Arizona lay in that direction — miles beyond the hills whose ragged contours looked deceptively smooth in the softening glow of the moon.

To the south was Mexico, a country with which he had become familiar, since Ben had seemed to have a liking for it — which, in turn, had compelled him to spend considerable time visiting its border settlements.

Once he had found himself deep in the hot wasteland known as the Chihuahua Desert, working his way to the mighty Sierra Madre range where Ben was being held captive by a band of Comancheros. At that time he'd gotten his first — and only — glimpse of his brother since embarking on the search, and he had thought then that the quest had come to an end.

It should have, just as it should have been a simple matter to overtake Ben after enabling him to escape the outlaws, but things had gone wrong and the hoped-for meeting never materialized. Had Ben been aware that it was his younger brother who made his escape possible the situation undoubtedly would have changed; but instead he had hurried on to cross the border and lose himself again in the wide, rugged reaches of the land where men could pass unnoticed and unquestioned as they drifted restlessly about on whatever personal mission occupied their lives.

Shawn pivoted slowly, moved slowly toward the sorrel. The strange reluctance was still upon him, and impatiently he brushed it aside. As well get down to the town, seek out Arlie Bishop, and learn what it was the lawman had to tell him about Ben.

Reaching the gelding, he stepped up into the saddle and settled himself, taking a moment, as always, to shift the holster filled with the worn forty-five Colt pistol carried on his left hip to a more comfortable and convenient position.

Satisfied, he cut the big horse about, crossed the meadow, and began to descend the gentle slope. The moon was now out in full face, laying a silver sheen upon the rocks and clothing the clumps of mountain mahogany and oak with a soft wooliness.

Far back on a ridge behind him a coyote yipped in its frantic, broken way, the call drawing an equally eerie reply from a kinsman nearby. And then from down in the distant town came the muffled report of gunshots, hollow but distinct in the warm night.

3

Starbuck frowned, but he did not slow the sorrel. The sound of gunshots in a settlement was no novelty and should not be particularly disturbing. There could be many explanations: a cowhand too deep in his whiskey and celebrating, a weapon's accidental discharge, someone killing a rattlesnake or other pestiferous varmint, a dispute in a card game, possibly.

There were numerous reasons, but for some cause unknown even to himself, an uneasiness had risen in Starbuck, and when at last the gelding reached the bottom of the slope and was on more secure footing, he raked the big horse with his rowels and put him into a fast lope for the town, less than a mile ahead in the valley.

He came to the end of the irregular street and pulled the sorrel back to a walk. More lamps in the windows of the stores along the dusty roadway had been lit, it seemed to him, and he reckoned that had something to do with the gunshots — which likely also accounted for the large number of people that were abroad.

Starbuck glanced about, eyes touching the signs marking the stores; Corrigan's Gun Shop, Grissom's General Store, the Blue Ribbon Bakery, Lone Star Cafe — a dozen other familiar and a few new, unfamiliar names. There were groups of people gathered on the porch of the Far West Hotel, a small assemblage in front of the Red Mule Saloon, and a larger crowd at its counterpart, the Valley Queen.

He saw a number of faces turn to him as he rode slowly on through the flooding lamplight. Many registered puzzled recognition, recalling him but not really remembering who he was. It was to be expected. He had been gone for four long years, and he had stayed among them for only a few days; then, too, people were prone to forget.

He came to the slight bend in the street and shifted on his saddle for a more comfortable position. His muscles ached from the full day of traveling, attempted purposely in order to reach Tannekaw by that evening. He'd be glad to be off the sorrel and set his feet on solid ground again.

The gelding began to slow of his own accord. A gathering of considerable size had collected in front of the jail. Evidently the gunshots had some connection with the law — with Arlie Bishop. Most likely the marshal had encountered trouble in jailing an arrested person, or perhaps there had been a jailbreak.

Shawn rode on past the crowd — all craning to see inside the marshal's office, where a dozen or more men had assembled — and circled to the side of the long, low building where he pulled to a halt at the hitch rack. Dismounting, he wrapped the sorrel's lines about the crossbar and doubled back to the street.

As he reached the fringe of the gathering there was a sudden commotion as a slim, dark man, somewhere in his mid-twenties and wearing a Deputy Marshal's star, pushed his way roughly through the pack to the doorway of the jail and disappeared inside.

A bystander to Shawn's left said, "Where you reckon Mulky's been?"

"Down at the Valley Queen, most likely. Where else?" a mocking voice replied from somewhere in the crowd.

"I seen him over around Ruby McGrath's," another man commented.

"Was told it was his job to keep a eye on Medford. Sure can't do that and be lollygagging with the girls at Ruby's!"

"Ain't that the truth!"

"Well, if he'd been on the job like he was

supposed to, maybe this here wouldn't've happened," the man to Starbuck's left observed in a serious tone. "Sure a hell of a note."

Shawn began to shoulder a path through the tight cluster of bystanders blocking his way to the door. A cowhand — from the looks of his clothing — swore as he came grudgingly around.

"Who the hell you think you are, shoving me?" he demanded, and then settled back as he got a full look at Starbuck's hard-set features.

A strong worry was flowing through Shawn. The words he'd overheard concerning the deputy, Mulky, the fact that the shooting had something to do with a prisoner supposedly locked in one of the cells, and Arlie Bishop being the marshal — all added up to something serious; and the answer was inside the jail.

Another onlooker wheeled angrily on him as he continued to bull his way through the crowd.

"Goddammit!" the man began, and then caught at Starbuck's arm. "Say — I recollect you from —"

Shawn, halted by the hand gripping his arm, nodded curtly. "Could be. I was here a few years back."

"Sure! Was you that stood by the marshal

against that bunch from the Longhorn Ranch. Your name's —"

"Starbuck," Shawn murmured, and jerking free, hurried on.

He reached the stoop fronting the jail, forced himself up onto it, and, entering the doorway, halted. The small office area was packed, and it still bore the smell of burnt gunpowder. Men were speaking in low voices and somewhere among them he could hear a woman weeping quietly.

He glanced about. Nearby was Grissom — still the mayor, he supposed. Gus Damson, who ran the livery stable, Hagerty of the Valley Queen, Albers, the hotel man, several who looked familiar but whose names he could not immediately recall, an equal number of strangers. And Doc Clay — Ed Clay.

Starbuck pushed deeper into the room, thrusting aside those who were in his path until he reached the physician. He had not noticed Clay at first glance, then he realized the man had been kneeling over someone stretched out on the floor and had just come upright. He dropped a hand on the older man's shoulder.

"Doc —"

Clay turned to him. A puzzled frown crossed the doctor's ruddy face briefly. He brushed at his gray shot mustache, finally nodded.

"Starbuck . . . Didn't know you were in town."

"Just rode up. What's this all about?"

"See for yourself," Clay replied, and reaching down, pulled back a blanket that had been laid over the figure on the floor.

Shawn stepped into the cleared space and glanced over the physician's shoulder. He stiffened. The man sprawled on the dusty floor was Arlie Bishop.

"He's been shot — dead," Ed Clay said.

4

For a long breath Starbuck studied the slack, lifeless features of the lawman, little changed from the last time he had seen him except for a full mustache; and then he looked up and glanced about. The woman he had heard weeping was Carla. She was sitting on a chair beyond Arlie's body. Face tipped down, dark hair glinting softly in the lamplight, she, too, appeared little different from four years back. He turned his attention to Clay.

"Heard the shots when I was up on the trail. What happened?"

"Ain't nobody sure," Gus Damson said before the doctor could reply. He broke off, leaned forward for a closer view of Shawn's features. "Ain't you that friend of Bishop's — Starbuck?"

"I am. Got word from him that he had something to tell me about my brother."

"He won't be telling nobody nothing," a voice cut in from somewhere near the doorway. There was a note of satisfaction in the speaker's tone, as if he had thought little of the lawman when he was alive.

Damson swore under his breath, flung an angry glance in the direction of the comment, and came back to Shawn.

"Was nobody around at the time. We all just heard shooting, come to see what it was about. Found the marshal laying there on the floor, dead. Whoever done it got out before anybody could see who he was."

"I had a look around town," Deputy Mulky said from the opposite side of the room. "Didn't spot nobody leaving in a hurry."

"Ain't likely you would," Grissom said dryly. "Was a good fifteen minutes before you showed up after the shots were fired."

"Yeh," someone said. "Just where the devil was you, Griff? Last I heard Bishop had give you orders to stand guard over Medford."

"What I was doing," the deputy declared sullenly. "But the marshal come in, told me to get out, go get myself a drink or something."

"Now, why'd he do that?" Grissom demanded disbelievingly.

"How would I know," Mulky shot back angrily. "I figured he had some private doings to take care of."

A moment of silence followed that, and then Rufe Hagerty said, "Could've been with the killer —"

"Like as not it was," Grissom said, nodding; "but what was it all about? I thought at first it was some of Case Medford's bunch come to break him out, but it sure don't look that way. Keys to the cell are still hanging there on the peg where Bishop always kept them — and Medford ain't gone."

Dr. Ed Clay glanced impatiently toward the door, muttering, "What the devil's keeping that undertaker?" Circling Arlie's body, he crossed to where Carla was sitting and glanced at a tall, light-haired man with pale eyes and a neat, clipped mustache standing behind her. He bobbed briskly at him, as if in dismissal.

"I'll look after her, Kerry," he said and laid his hand on the woman's shoulder. The tall man merely fell back a half step.

"You figure there's any use mounting a posse and trying to run down the killer?" Albers wondered. "Seems we ought to be doing something besides just standing around."

"Ain't much we can do while it's dark," Deputy Griff Mulky said, shrugging.

"Moon's plenty bright —"

"Ain't bright enough to do no tracking by, and that's all we'll have to go on — tracks," Mulky said. He added, "Couple a hundred different ones around here by now — and we ain't got no idea which way that killer headed when he left here. Going to be hard to figure which set of tracks to follow — if we can find some that ain't been all tromped to hell."

Starbuck, standing silent in the midst of the crowd filling the stuffy, packed room, listened to the comments being made. He was saying nothing, simply allowing himself, as was his habit, to collect the available facts and pertinent information that was to be had, storing everything in his mind before offering to take a hand.

Damson said, "The deputy's right, I expect. We plain got to come up with something else."

"You study out why it was the marshal got hisself shot, then maybe we can get a idea of just who it was that done it," a voice in the crowd suggested. "Was I guessing, I'd say it was one of Medford's bunch."

Again a hush fell over the lawman's quarters as if all present were giving the thought consideration. It had grown exceedingly warm in the small confines of the jail, and the shine of sweat now lay on the faces of most who were there. Doc Clay had dropped to a crouch beside Carla Bishop and was talking to her quietly. She had not raised her head, but simply continued to stare at her clasped hands, resting in her lap.

Starbuck turned to Damson. "Keep hearing the name Medford mentioned —"

The stableman nodded. "Outlaw — a real bad one. Bishop's got him locked up in the back. He was aiming to take him to Clayton City, hand him over to Sheriff Saffire for the bounty money that's on him — five thousand dollars."

"Lot of cash," Shawn murmured.

"Yeh, but like I said, Medford's a bad one. Him and his gang've been raising hell around here and points east for a year or better — specially with the stagecoaches. Even robbed a few trains over in Kansas and Missouri, I hear tell."

"You know, I was just thinking it could've been some bounty hunter hoping to get his paws on Medford that shot down the marshal," added Albers, after listening to the livery stable owner's explanation. "That five thousand reward's probably got every bounty hunter west of the Missouri looking for Case Medford."

Damson scrubbed at the stubble on his jaw. "Could have been," he admitted. "But like Henry Grissom said, the cell keys ain't been touched, and somebody wanting to get his hands on Medford so bad that he'd kill the marshal would've tried to get him out of that cell."

"Unless something — or somebody — scared him off before he could do it."

Damson continued to claw at his chin, nodding slowly. "You just maybe've got something there, Clint. There could've been somebody out there in the street that was coming this way. Drove the killer off before he had time to get Medford out."

"There ain't nobody stepped up and said they seen somebody in the street," a man standing behind Damson said. "Or leaving the jail, either."

"No proof there wasn't," Albers countered. "Folks get sort of absent-minded at times, pay no attention to what's going on around them."

"But them gunshots —"

"I ain't saying they wasn't heard. Only that maybe whoever it was in the street — if there was somebody — just didn't think about it and kept on going to wherever they was headed. Anyways, gunshots ain't all that unusual, not with that Longhorn bunch blowing off every now and then."

"Well, I sure'n hell didn't see nobody, going or coming," the man declared, unconvinced; "and I was one of the first to get here."

"That ain't hard to understand," Albers said. "How long did it take for you to figure out where the shots came from and for you to get here?"

"Four, maybe five minutes —"

"Exactly. A man's in his house. He hears shooting and goes outside to see what's going on, if he even bothers at all. Unless there's somebody standing in the middle of the street holding a gun in his hand, a fellow can't tell where the shots came from until he does some looking around."

"Expect you're right," Gus Damson agreed thoughtfully. "If there was somebody in the street that scared the killer off after he shot Bishop, he could've been clear out of town by the time we got the gunshots located."

"You talking about the killer or somebody passing by?" It was the man who had arrived first on the scene. He was still skeptical.

"About somebody passing by —"

Albers swiped at the sweat on his face. "I reckon it'd pay to start asking everybody living close around here if they seen anybody on the street about the time it happened. Just might turn up something."

The crowd in Bishop's office had begun to thin out, as had that gathered outside. The first blush of excitement was over and there was now nothing left to do but return home, or to one of the saloons, and rehash and speculate on the incident.

"What are we going to do about Medford, Henry?" Hagerty asked, putting his question to Tannekaw's mayor. "Bishop was planning to move him out tomorrow."

Grissom ran fingers through his thin, graying hair. "Well, I sure don't want him around here any longer'n necessary. I'll try to line up somebody to take him to Clayton City."

"Could use the deputy —"

"Nope, I don't want the town without a lawman, leastwise not the way things are right now. . . . And I think what Gus Damson and Clint Albers was saying there a couple of minutes ago makes sense. We ought to begin asking folks if they seen somebody on the street. Mulky can start the morning off doing that — I'll get Medford to Clayton City somehow."

"You ain't apt to find no volunteers," Albers said. "Nobody'll want that job."

"Smart thing'll be to sort of sneak him out," someone suggested.

"I'll figure something," Grissom said confidently.

Starbuck had continued to listen to the exchange quietly, letting it all register while he got a clear picture of what had, and was, taking place. He had made no further mention of the reason for his presence in Tannekaw — and he reckoned he could forget it, at least where Arlie Bishop himself was concerned.

There was a good chance, however, that Griff Mulky knew what it was the lawman wanted to tell him. He'd hold off until later — next morning, perhaps — when he could talk with the deputy without a crowd being around. And Carla — he should also speak with her. Arlie could have mentioned it to her.

He half turned at the sound of heels in the doorway. Two men, one bearing a stretcher, were entering. Doc Clay immediately drew himself upright, crossed to where Bishop lay.

"Took you long enough," he said grumpily to the older of the pair.

The undertaker shrugged. "Was old Mrs. Calloway. She passed on a couple hours ago. Was out at her place, busy," he explained. He motioned to his assistant — evidently a son, as there was a strong family resemblance — to place the stretcher beside Bishop's body.

Together they lifted the lawman, laid him on the stretcher, and with the blanket still covering him, took positions between the wooden poles, came upright, and hurried out into the street.

Starbuck shifted his attention to Carla, suddenly feeling the push of her eyes upon him. As their glances locked, he nodded slightly. Immediately Carla smiled, and ignoring the tall man behind her, rose and moved across the now near deserted room to him.

"How are you, Shawn?" she asked, extending a hand.

He took her slender fingers into his. "Fine. Mighty sorry about Arlie."

Carla's eyes were red from weeping. She lowered her head quickly, was silent as she struggled to recover herself. That accomplished after the lapse of several moments, she again faced him.

"I'm still having trouble believing it. It's so hard to think that —"

"I want you to go home and get some rest," Doc Clay cut in brusquely. "You've been through a big strain. Now, I can give you something to make you sleep, if you like."

"I won't need it," Carla said, shaking her head, and turned her attention to Henry Grissom and the few others yet remaining. "Thank you all for what you've done."

"Wasn't much," the town's mayor replied. "And I reckon we all forgot to tell you we're sorry about it. Your husband was a fine man."

Grissom hadn't always felt that way about Arlie Bishop, Starbuck thought. Evidently things had changed, and for the better.

Albers said, tentatively, "Now, if there's anything we can do —"

"I'll be all right," Carla said. "Shawn will see me home." She came about, faced the man addressed as Kerry. "He was our — Arlie's and my — best friend, Dave."

Kerry nodded, thrust a hand toward Starbuck. "Glad you happened by," he said.

Shawn accepted the tall man's firm grip. Dave Kerry was well dressed, had the smooth, cool manner of a professional gambler, and appeared to regard Carla Bishop with an air of possessiveness. He had evidently intended to see to her needs, was taken aback by her statement.

At once Starbuck stepped aside, allowed Carla to move by him for the door, and then, following her out into the street, took her by the arm and pointed toward the house to the rear of the jail where he recalled the Bishops lived.

"Same place?" he asked, hesitating.

"The same," she answered.

5

Abe Ladner, sitting in the half dark at the rear of the Red Mule Saloon, rocked back in his chair and gave the buxom, gaudily dressed girl who paused at the table an appreciative head to toe scrutiny. A dark, swarthy man with curly hair and laughing eyes, he had little trouble making friends with the ladies. After a moment, he grinned.

"Come set, sister," he said, reaching out for the girl. "You're the kind I take a real fancy to. What's your name?"

"Jackie," she replied, moving in and sitting down on his knee. "What's yours?"

"Can call me Abe —"

The two men opposite Ladner at the table watched in silence for a time and then one, a redhead with light, flat eyes and a ruddy complexion, swore angrily.

"Goddammit, Abe — can't you think of nothing but a woman?" he demanded in an exasperated voice.

Ladner, pulling the girl close, roving hands all the while exploring her body, smiled broadly. “You figure out anything better to be doing, Mister Rockmond?”

“Right now I sure’s hell can,” the redhead snapped, and rising, took Jackie by the arm, pulled her upright, and shoved her none too gently toward the bar. “Beat it, girlie. We got some private talking to do.”

Abe frowned and his dark features flushed. He came partly to his feet. “Just you hold on a goddam minute here! I can do —”

Rockmond waved the younger man back. “Set down,” he ordered, flatly. “Me and Dow’s got something to say. When we’re done you can grab yourself that gal and half a dozen others and trot off to bed if you’re of a mind.”

Ladner settled back, eyes still glowing with anger. Dow, the third member of the party, a balding, hawk-faced man somewhere in his forties, reached for the bottle in front of him and refilled the glasses.

“The marshall’s dead,” he said, putting his glance on Ladner. “That’s what all that hoorawing out in the street was about.”

Abe, ignoring the drink set before him, took a swallow direct from the bottle. “So he’s dead. Ain’t going to change nothing far as Case is concerned.”

“Could change it a’plenty,” Rockmond snapped impatiently. “If you’d a gone with us instead of staying here fiddling with every skirt that you could lay your paws on, you'd know that."

Ladner's shoulders stirred indifferently. "They still got to take him to Clayton City, and that's all we give a damn about."

"It's liable to be different. Way they was planning it, that Marshal Bishop was doing the taking. They'll be coming up with a new plan now."

"Good chance that sheriff at Clayton'll come after Medford. Could even be bringing a U.S. Marshal with him, if he does."

Ladner again shrugged. "So?"

"Means we best change our plans."

"Why? Three of us, and if the sheriff shows up with a U.S. Marshal, the odds'll still be with us. Can't see where we'll have any trouble busting old Case loose. By God, you two are like a couple of old hens fussing over their chicks —"

"I ain't aiming to slip up," Rockwood said quietly. "We promised Case we'd get the law off him, and we're going to do it."

"Sure we are," Ladner drawled. "I ain't thinking on nothing else, and the sooner we do, the better I'll be liking it. I'm about out of money, and that there bank Case was figuring on us emptying when he got hisself caught sounded like a mighty easy deal."

"It is," Dow said, "long as Case is there to call the shots. It'll have to wait 'til he is, so don't go getting any ideas. He's the only one that knows how it can be done."

"If we'd been smart we'd made him tell us all about it so's we could be doing it while —"

"Case Medford ain't the kind you make do nothing," the red-headed Rockmond said dryly. "I figured you knew that."

Abe made no reply. Dow, refilling his glass again, began to twirl it gently between a thumb and forefinger, eyes half closed. Elsewhere in the saloon the piano player had struck up a tune and several couples had gathered in the small, cleared area reserved for dancing and were swaying and stomping to the beat of the music.

"What me and Red's been wondering about — and we best try to figure — is who was it that plugged the marshal, and why," Dow said finally, looking up.

"Who the hell cares?" Abe commented, watching the dancers closely. "Makes no nevermind to us."

"It sure better!" Rockmond said. "There's a'plenty a folks around here think maybe it was a bounty hunter looking to grab off Case and trot him off to some other John Law and claim the reward they're paying."

Ladner frowned, brought his attention

back to his friends. "That what you think?"

"I ain't thinking nothing for certain," the redhead stated. "Only trying to get things lined up so's we don't find ourselves in a picklement."

Abe Ladner slumped deeper into his chair. "Well, if that's what the shooting was all about, it didn't work. Case's still there in that cage just like he's been for nigh onto a week, ain't he?"

"Yeh, but the point is we maybe've got more'n whoever it is that'll be taking him to Clayton City to worry about. Could be a whole bunch of bounty hunters are hanging around, waiting to cash in on Cash. That's a lot of money — five thousand dollars."

Abe stroked his mustache, nodded. "Chance of that, all right. Hadn't give it no thought."

"It's what Dow and me are trying to get in your head if you'll forget them women for a few minutes!" Red said, raising his voice to be heard above the thumping of the dancers. "This here could be serious."

Ladner sighed heavily. "I'm listening. What're we going to do?"

"First off we best do some smelling around, see if there is a bounty hunter — maybe several, or even a gang of them — hanging around waiting to grab Case."

"How'll we know?"

"Could be somebody you'll recognize. There ain't so many of them running loose that you'll be stepping on them."

"They got a look to them," Dow agreed. "Can spot them easy."

"Won't be no big chore," Abe said. "Then what?"

"We got to find out soon as we can what they're aiming to do about Case. If they're letting that deputy take him to Clayton City, we got no problem. If they hold him for the sheriff or some U.S. Marshal, that's a mule with a longer tail."

"Why?" Ladner wondered. "Ain't never yet seen a one of them with a hide so thick it'd stop a bullet."

"Not the problem. They'll like as not have a different scheme and maybe won't be taking Case through the mountains to Clayton City. Could line out for some other town. And they could load him into a stagecoach instead of horseback."

"And they could deputize themselves a half a dozen men to ride along — sort of a escort," Dow pointed out. "That'd make it plenty tough."

Rockmond nodded. "For a fact. We had us a cinch deal with that marshal, Bishop, taking Case. He was aiming to do it alone."

"Would've been like shooting fish in a barrel," Dow said. "That jasper was mighty proud of hisself."

Rockmond swore disconsolately. "Might've known something would go wrong — was all too easy. But there ain't no use bawling over it. We just got to change things to fit. Right now we best start moving around, doing some listening and finding out what's what.

"There's two more saloons in this burg — the Valley Queen where all the range bulls do their drinking, and a little ragtag joint called the Silver Dollar. We'll split up, one of us staying here, the others going to the Silver Dollar and the Valley Queen. We'll just sort of stall around, see if we can spot us them bounty hunters, and at the same time do some listening, learn what the town's planning to do with Case."

"I'll stick around here," Abe said. "Be easy for me to get that little gal, Jackie, to do some nosing about —"

"You ain't telling her nothing!" Red cut in sharply. "Hear? She'll go asking questions about why you're wanting to know — and then it'll be all over town who we are and why we're here."

Abe's jaw tightened and a glint came into his eyes. "Hell, I ain't that dumb, Red. I ain't about to show my cards to her or nobody else."

Rockmond snorted. "You get to fooling around with a woman and she can worm anything she wants out of you! I've seen it done! All she's got to do is wiggle her hind-end and pull down the front of her dress and you start gabbling like an old turkey gobbler!"

"The hell —"

"Red's right," Dow said. "You got to keep your lady friends out of this."

"Thinking about it," Rockmond stated suddenly, "you best don't do nothing — just leave it all up to Dow and me. You set right here, have yourself a good time. We've had us a look around this dump anyway and we ain't seen nobody special."

"Ain't likely to hear nothing neither," Dow added.

"Not that we're needing to hear. Me and Dow'll go hang around them other saloons, see what we can come up with. Now, you think you can set here and keep your trap shut about us while we're gone?"

The anger and indignation had faded swiftly from Abe Ladner. A broad smile now parted his heavy mouth.

"Something I can do real good, pardner," he said, and raising a hand, he beckoned to one of the girls.

6

The house appeared little different after four years. Only a hundred yards or so to the west of the jail, it was a small, pitched-roof, square-built structure — and still in need of a coat of paint. Nestled between two large, spreading cottonwoods, it had a settled, comfortable look.

They walked the short distance in silence, and upon reaching there, Carla crossed the front porch, opened the door, and led Starbuck into the parlor. A bead-trimmed lamp placed in the center of a circular library table had been lit and its glow filled the room, pointing up the lacy antimacassars gracing the furniture, the flowered wallpaper, and the half dozen family portraits hung in ornate frames.

"Jeannie's in bed," Carla said, finally breaking her silence as Shawn glanced expectantly toward a hallway leading to the rear of the house. Looking down, she shook her head. "I — I don't think I'll wake her to tell her about Arlie. It can wait 'til morning. . . . Would you like some coffee?"

"Go mighty good, if it's no trouble," Starbuck replied, and following her into the kitchen, sat down on one of the straight-back chairs placed about the table where the family apparently took their meals.

"What brought you to Tannekaw?" Carla asked, poking the coals in the cook stove into life and adding a few sticks of kindling. "I never thought to see you again, Shawn."

He was watching her as she went about the simple chore of warming the coffee. Carla had lost none of her beauty; indeed, the years had supplied strength and character to it. Where it had once been of a delicate, sheltered type, it was now strong and vital.

"To see Arlie."

She paused, turned, leveled her eyes — darker blue in the light of the lamp bracketed on a wall — at him.

"Why?"

"Got word he wanted to see me. Was something about my brother — about him being —"

"Are you still looking for him?" Carla interrupted in surprise.

Starbuck nodded. "Stagecoach driver had been told to leave word for me along the line. He had it that Ben, my brother, was dead, and that I was to see Arlie about it."

Carla turned back to the stove. "I'm sorry

to hear that," she murmured as she took up the coffeepot and shook it gently, gauging the amount of its contents. Judging there was a sufficiency, she placed it over the firebox and, coming back around, sat down opposite him.

"How long ago was this?"

"I got the word only a few days ago. Don't know when Arlie put it out. Could've been months. Did he say anything to you about it?"

Carla brushed at a stray lock of hair. "No, nothing," she said and lowered her eyes. "But that isn't unusual. Arlie and I haven't been very close for the last year or so."

Shawn offered no comment. Earlier, at the jail, he had wondered about the Bishops. Carla had appeared only moderately affected by Arlie's death, but he had put it down as shock.

"Arlie changed so," she continued. "He was not at all the man you knew. The job — being town marshal — just sort of went to his head after that first year, and he got to where he could think of nothing but money."

"I remember he was dead set on making something of himself," Starbuck said. "Told me once he'd never had anything and had never amounted to anything but he was sure going to try and change that. He worried a lot about providing for you and the little girl."

"It didn't work out exactly that way," Carla said, sighing.

The lid on the granite coffeepot had begun to tremble from steam building up inside, and rising, Carla took two cups from a shelf, set them on the table, and filled them with coffee. In the quiet of the room, now fragrant with the good, homey odor of the freshly poured brew, Shawn glanced idly about.

"House sure looks nice —"

"I love it," Carla said, returning to her chair. "I've enjoyed living here, and we were happy for a while. Then Arlie began to change, as I've already said — but let's not talk about that. It's so good to see you again, Shawn. You look just the same — a bit older perhaps, but that's all to the good."

"The years coming are something you can't sidestep. Not much difference in the way you looked four years ago."

Carla smiled. "I'll take that as a compliment. Haven't you been able to even get close to your brother in all this time?"

"Near enough once to get a look at him, but not to do any talking."

Carla sipped at her coffee. Then: "Seems by now, with you leaving word here and there, he'd know you were trying to find him and make an effort to meet you."

A hard smile parted Starbuck's lips. "I get

the idea every once in awhile that he doesn't want that."

Carla stared at him. "Why?"

"Probably thinks I've been sent by Pa to patch things up between them and talk him into going back home with me. I doubt if he knows Pa's dead. And far as me leaving word for him, having Arlie send for me is the first time it's ever worked. Of all the folks I've asked to pass it on — lawmen, bartenders, ranchers, store owners — he's the first one."

Carla was quiet for a long breath. "Arlie thought a lot of you, Shawn," she said, finally. "He never forgot all that you did for him — us."

"Only what any man would do for another needing a hand."

"I'm not too sure of that, and it caused you to miss out on seeing Ben, didn't it? I remember Arlie saying that you thought he was in some town nearby at the time but you stayed here anyway until everything was all right for us."

Shawn took a swallow of his coffee. "Didn't know he knew about that."

"He found out later from somebody. . . . I wish I could tell you what it was he wanted, but he never mentioned it. You might look through the papers in his desk. There could be a letter or something. And you should talk to Griff Mulky about it."

"Figured to do that."

"Like as not Griff won't be much help. He hated Arlie."

Starbuck frowned. "Hated him — why?"

"Arlie was hard to get along with. He made Griff stay close to the jail, do all the work around town while he'd go off after some outlaw who had a price on his head. Griff felt he should have a share of the rewards that Arlie collected."

"That true with this Case Medford, too? Was told the bounty on him is five thousand dollars."

"Specially him. Griff and Arlie had a bad argument over him. Griff wanted half of what was being paid — but Arlie refused to give him any of it, not one dollar. He told Griff that a deputy was supposed to be satisfied with what he got as wages."

Starbuck gave that thought. Then: "Expect you've been asked this already, but have you got any idea who could have killed Arlie?"

Carla sloshed the remainder of her coffee about in her cup slowly. "You're wondering if it was Griff. I don't know. He could have been angry enough to do it, and I suppose he's capable of such a thing. As for others, Arlie made plenty of enemies — he was bound to, being town marshal and using his authority the way he did. He was terribly hard on a lot of men, some that deserved it and a few who didn't."

Arlie Bishop really had changed, Shawn thought, and looking back, recalling the man as he had known him, it was difficult to believe; but such a transition was not necessarily unusual, he knew. Many men, unaccustomed to authority and having themselves been cowed by it in the past, go to extremes once they hold power in their own hands.

"Are you going to stay in Tannekaw a while?"

Carla's question brought Starbuck back to the moment. "Hard to say. I'd like to see if anybody else around knows what it is that Arlie wanted to tell me. I'm hoping that stagecoach driver had it wrong about Ben being dead, of course. Can you think of anybody else besides the deputy that Arlie might have talked to about it?"

Carla said, "No, not that I know of. Arlie just wasn't on very good terms with anybody."

Shawn recalled the tall, dark man who had been hovering near Carla. "What about this fellow Kerry? Acts like he was sort of a family friend."

"Dave? Yes, he's a friend, all right," she said slowly. "I don't think Arlie liked him much, although he never said so, or even showed it — at least when I was around."

"Who is he, anyway?"

"Came here from somewhere in the south, I think. Educated, very nice, and has plenty of money. Does some gambling, I was told. I think one reason Arlie didn't care for him was that he's what Arlie would like to be — or would have liked, I guess I'd better say."

"Meaning?"

"Oh, well-dressed, tall, good-looking, money — the sort that other people like to talk to and be seen with."

"Arlie had you. Seems that'd be enough for any man."

Carla smiled. "Thank you, Shawn. I only wish it had been true."

"Where does this Dave Kerry get his money?"

Carla Bishop shrugged. "I have no idea. Family, I guess." She hesitated, frowned. "Asking all these questions about him — you surely don't think he could have shot . . ."

"Not thinking anything much," Starbuck replied. "I haven't been around and don't know what the score on anybody is. Just trying to get it all in my head," he added and pushed back from the table. "Reckon I best be going, let you get some rest."

Carla rose with him. "I doubt I'll have any

trouble. It's been a long day."

"And a hard one for you, I expect. Appreciate your telling the little girl hello for me. She wasn't but a button when I last saw her."

"Three years old — and I'll tell her. You'll be around tomorrow though, won't you?"

"Sure."

"I'll see you?"

"Can bet on it," Starbuck said, turning for the door. "Don't bother to see me out — I can find my own way. Good night."

"Good night, Shawn," Carla murmured.

7

It was sad to learn of the change in Arlie Bishop, particularly where he and Carla were concerned, Starbuck thought as he walked slowly along the path that led back to town. He had believed the most important thing in life to the lawman was his wife and their small daughter.

But there was no hard and fast rule decreeing a man must not change, for the better or for worse, and the driving desire to have money was more often than not a cruel taskmaster. Arlie, by his own admission, had been a penniless, consistent failure; it was not difficult to understand how he could fall victim to ruthless ambition.

Shawn slowed, swore quietly, came to a halt. In his surprise at hearing of the present-day Arlie Bishop, he had neglected to offer his assistance to Carla in making funeral arrangements. It was only common decency — and the oversight should be rectified. He glanced over his shoulder to the house. It wasn't too late; light still showed in the windows. Like as not Carla was still in the kitchen doing whatever chores were left undone when the word came of her husband's death.

Wheeling, Starbuck began to retrace his steps up the slight grade. He reached the edge of the yard, then drew to a sudden stop. There was movement in the shadows at the side of the house.

A frown pulled at Shawn's features and his hand dropped to the pistol at his hip. It could be the killer. Having squared a fancied or real grudge with Arlie, he perhaps intended to fulfill his need for complete vengeance by murdering the rest of the Bishop family.

Abruptly tense, Starbuck drew off to one side and faded into the blackness cast by the thickly leafed trees. Careful, he moved toward the point where he had seen the intruder, all the while listening intently into the still night, heavy with the scent of lilac bushes in bloom.

Dogs were barking somewhere along the north fringe of town for some cause, and back among the houses that lay just beyond its street a woman's voice was calling a child home. Overhead, through the limbs of the cottonwoods, stars were visible; and in the open where there was no hindrance, moonlight flooded the land.

A twig snapped. Shawn froze, hand again riding the butt of his forty-five. The sound had come from his left, from the bushes that grew along the side of the house where they had been planted as a windbreak.

Motionless, Starbuck waited. Whoever it was would need to cross a narrow strip of yard to reach the building from where he presently was. The door opening into the kitchen was on that side and directly opposite. Anyone doing so would be in full, unobstructed view.

Lamplight abruptly filled the rectangle of a window farther along the wall. One of the bedrooms, Shawn recalled. Probably that of the little girl, Jeannie.

The window remained aglow for a long minute, and then went dark again with only the yellowish reflection of the moon showing on the glass to mark its location. Carla had evidently gone into her small daughter's room to assure herself that all was well.

Movement in the shadows once again caught Shawn's attention. The intruder now appeared to be making his way toward the rear of the house, doing so quietly and with great care. At once Starbuck began to follow, equally cautious. The intruder reached the corner of the structure, rounded it, crossed over, started a slow return up the opposite side.

Now thoroughly puzzled, Shawn continued to stalk the man. Was he, whoever he was, simply making certain there was no one nearby before he made his move? Or was he some friend of the Bishops', having the same thought of the killer's further vengeance on the family and taking it upon himself to see that no harm came to Carla and her daughter?

It could be Griff Mulky. A deputy filled with consideration for the man he had served under would undoubtedly take measures to protect that man's remaining relatives until the killer was found and brought in — only Mulky would not qualify for such; Carla had said the deputy and Arlie didn't get along, that Griff actually hated the lawman. That would certainly eliminate Mulky.

The slow, tedious circuit of the house was completed. They were again in the windbreak facing the kitchen. Starbuck, steadily growing impatient but unwilling to take any action until he knew what he was up against, rode out the dragging minutes. If the intruder was a friend of the Bishops' he didn't want to be guilty of challenging him — but if the opposite were true . . .

Abruptly a tall shape stepped from the windbreak. In a half a dozen long strides he crossed to the door. There he paused, a taut figure in the pale glow, for a full breath; then raising an arm, he rapped softly.

Starbuck eased in nearer, suspicion still

having its upper hand with him. . . . A young and beautiful woman, now a widow, alone in a house except for a sleeping child — a strong temptation for some men. One had but to knock, and when the summons was answered, force his way inside.

The door opened. Carla stood framed in the light flooding out into the yard — and pointing up the features of the man. It was Dave Kerry.

"Looked around good, didn't see anybody," Shawn heard him say. "Just wanted to be certain."

Carla made a reply, inaudible to Starbuck, and stepped back. Kerry, removing his flat-crowned hat, moved forward to enter.

He spoke more words as he disappeared into the house, but they were lost to Shawn when the door closed behind him. Chagrined, Starbuck turned back into the shrubbery. He'd blundered into a clandestine meeting between Carla Bishop and Kerry, who, it would appear, was indeed a friend of the family's — particularly Carla's. But that was their business, not his. She had said that matters had not been right where she and Arlie were concerned. Evidently Carla had filled that void with Dave Kerry.

Starbuck paused as a thought came into his mind. Could there be an affair of such proportions existing between Dave Kerry and Carla, an affair so serious that he would murder Arlie Bishop to simplify the situation for them?

Shawn's jaw hardened. If that were true, then it *was* his business.

8

Tildy Cobb — stringy, unkempt hair hanging stiffly about her angular shoulders, patched, nondescript dress worn to colorless gray after years of constant wear sagging about her bony frame — shifted the cud of tobacco in her thin-lipped mouth and glared at the two boys sitting opposite her across the kitchen table. They were on a crude bench while she occupied the sole chair in the dusty, littered room.

"You telling me for true?" she demanded in a harsh, cracked voice. A woman, long widowed, had to be firm in raising sons. If you wasn't, they'd walk the hell all over you.

"Yes'm," Eustace, the older of the pair replied, nodding vigorously.

Light-haired, brown-eyed, and slim, he took after her, Tildy reckoned. Billy, on the other hand, just turned seventeen and two years his brother's junior, was dark like his pa, Vic, had been.

Tildy turned and spat an amber stream into the dirt box placed alongside the cook stove for such purpose.

"Well, dammit, talk up — tell me about it! I was figuring you'd be here with Case Medford a'trailing behind you, grinning happy. Instead you showed up with nothing."

"We didn't have no chance, Ma," Billy said. "We was there, just like we had it all planned out — waiting and watching from the dark, looking for us a chance to get in that jail and get Case . . ."

"I was aiming to take care of the deputy," Eustace cut in. "Had me a pisselm club all ready to use on his head —"

"And I was aiming to grab me up the keys and let Medford out, only —"

Tildy leaned back in the chair, hard, old, unforgiving eyes drilling into the boys like flint points. Neither one of them had ever been worth a damn, but a body did the best they could with what the good Lord seen fit to provide. Only why in the hell couldn't one of them've been a smidgin like their pa — an honest-to-God man?

"Only," she prompted impatiently, and again bathed the dirt box.

"Was another fellow beat us to it."

Tildy came bolt upright. "You saying somebody else busted out Case Medford?"

"No'm, don't mean that."

"Then what the goddam hell do you mean?"

"Some jaybird showed up right about when we got ready to make our move. Went inside the jail, and next thing we knew there was shooting."

"He shot Case?"

"No'm — the marshal. Killed him deader'n a fence post."

Tildy settled back, relieved. "Oh, had me fearing it was Case that got killed. Who was this here jasper?"

"Don't know," Eustace replied. "The sonofabitch —"

"Don't you cuss in front of me, boy!"

Eustace squirmed. "You cuss . . ."

"I'm your ma. I got a right. Just you keep remembering that, hear?"

"Yes'm."

"Now, what about that fellow?"

"Couldn't tell who he was. Had on one of them long shiny coats."

"A slicker."

"Yes'm. Soon as he shot the marshal he come running out and ducked into the dark 'longside the building. Was plenty gone before folks started showing up to see what the shooting was all about."

"We sort've hung around 'til we knowed what was what, then we hightailed back here."

Tildy Cobb nodded in satisfaction. "Just

so's it weren't Case that got plugged. Be no chance of us collecting that reward then."

Billy glanced hopefully toward the stove. "They anything to eat, Ma? I'm hungrier'n a bull calf with his throat cut."

Tildy gestured toward a blackened pot sitting on the back of the battered old range. Like everything else around the place it had long since seen better times, and it stood now precariously propped on a flat rock and three legs.

"Beans and sowbelly there. Be some cornbread in the oven."

The younger Cobb boy groaned. "I mighty sick of sowbelly and beans," he declared in a falling voice. "Can't we never have no chicken or rabbit or something else?"

"We got about a dozen hens left, and we can't eat them and expect them to lay eggs, too — and rabbit's got plumb scarce lately," Tildy said. "You eat beans and sowbelly or do without."

"Yes, Ma," the boy muttered truculently, and rising, he trudged to the stove.

"Ain't you hungry?" Tildy asked, setting her eyes on Eustace.

"Reckon so," he answered with no enthusiasm, and coming to his feet, he joined his brother, filling a wooden bowl from the pot of the constantly replenished and cornmeal-thickened concoction.

"It ain't always going to be like this," Tildy said. "Better times are a'coming."

Vic had quoted those identical words to her, Tildy recalled, and he'd done everything he could to make the prophecy come true.

She'd first met him in a Kansas City saloon where she was working. After a night in the loft he'd told her right straight out he wanted her to come along with him. He didn't have nothing, he'd made that plain, but he was aiming to. It'd just take a mite of time.

She had listened to him and accepted, and he'd even married her, doing it all legal and proper with a circuit-riding Methodist preacher saying the words. Not that Vic had to go that far; hell, she would've gone to hell with a busted back for him if he'd wanted — he was that kind of a man. They'd took off and tramped about the country for a spell after that — for about four years, in fact, with Vic doing one thing and another to keep them in eating money. Then along had come Eustace, and almost before she could think to count the months, there was Billy.

The boys had kind of changed Vic. He got more serious and tried harder to get things shaped up right for her and them. One day when they were about five or six or thereabouts, he'd come home real pleased and grinning like a possum eating hornets. He had the deed to a ranch — a place where they could settle down and raise the boys the way folks was supposed to, he'd said.

Vic didn't explain how he'd come by the ranch, a hundred and sixty acres about ten miles outside a town called Tannekaw. It had been a bet he'd won, that was all he'd say, and Tildy let it go at that.

It was no fluke. The place was theirs, and while it sure wasn't much, it was home — a house, chicken yard, pigpen, sheds for cows and horses. They didn't have any cash to do much improving, but that would come, Vic said, and they both of them worked like a couple of field hands trying to get the place to going.

Luck didn't favor them, hardly. They did manage to eat, get themselves a couple a dozen chickens and four hogs. They had horses, old Jack and Brownie, the team they'd used to pull the buckboard they'd done their traveling in. There never had been enough money to buy a cow.

Finally things got so bad, work being the way it was — just about none at all — that Vic up and said one night he was damn tired of slaving, that he was going out and get them some money by whichever how he could.

He rode off on Brownie that next morning,

telling her not to fret, that she'd hear from him mighty soon. She did, too. About a month later a letter came for her. There was forty dollars in it and a note from him saying there'd be more soon. He'd throwed in with a half a dozen fellows he'd known back in Missouri and they expected to be doing real well.

Tildy hadn't questioned what Vic and his friends might be doing to earn that money. Getting it was all that counted and she'd made the best of what looked like a godsend by purchasing a cow, a few more chickens, paper and tar to repair the leaky roof of the house, and laying in a big stock of food. She had also squandered five whole dollars on sensible work overalls and heavy shoes for the boys and a dress for herself.

That was the last she ever heard from Vic himself. One day several months later a man rode by. Said he was a friend of Vic's and that he was real sorry to bring her bad news but he'd made a promise that he was bounden to keep. Vic had got himself killed. Well, it was during a stagecoach holdup. Here was Vic's belongings — pistol, holster, cartridge belt, and the three dollars he'd had in his pocket. Vic was a good old boy, the rider had declared, and everybody sure did like him. Was too bad he got ventilated. They'd buried him right there on the spot.

Tildy had accepted the news and Vic's possessions with a great sense of loss and desolation. She'd gone off into the room she'd shared with him, thrown herself on the bed, and cried like a baby. Then it was over. It was all up to her now. She had to keep on living and raising the two younguns. Vic would have told her so if he could've.

Thus the struggle began, a hand-to-mouth existence that offered little future until one day she heard that Case Medford, a man she and Vic had once been friends with in Kansas, was right there in the Tannekaw jail waiting to be taken to the sheriff at Clayton City, up north of them aways. The marshal had caught Case and was aiming to collect a five-thousand-dollar bounty for turning him over to that Clayton City sheriff.

Five thousand dollars! God in heaven, what she could do with that much money! Fix the place up proper like it should be, buy some cattle . . . Vic always had wanted to raise cattle. He'd wanted it so bad that she'd once approached him with the suggestion that with all the herds grazing loose around the country, it'd be no chore at all to just help themselves to a few; a couple at a time, they'd sure never be missed. But Vic had said no. Quickest way to a hanging tree was rustling stock, he'd told her. Man maybe could turn to stealing other things, but he sure better leave another fellow's cattle be.

There'd be plenty to buy stock now, get some decent clothes for the boys, now grown and turning into men, and for herself. She was still wearing the dress she'd bought with part of that forty dollars. . . . And food — hell almighty, they could eat like rich folks!

So Tildy Cobb had come up with a simple scheme. The boys would slip into town one night, enter the jail, and get Case Medford. He'd come along with them when they told them who they were — Vic and Tildy Cobb's boys — and that they were there to help him.

They'd then bring him to the house. She'd be waiting with a gun and a rope. They'd make Case their prisoner, load him onto the buckboard, and haul him across the line into Arizona where she'd hand him over to the first sheriff she could find — and collect herself five thousand dollars jingling dollars for her trouble. Lord, Lord, they'd be rich! They could live high on the hog for the rest of their lives!

Tildy became aware of her two sons. They had finished the sowbelly and beans, were now sucking noisily at tin cups filled with chicory while waiting for her to tell them what next to do. That was always the way of it; it was forever up to her to do the thinking —

and too damn much of the time, the doing. Hell, neither one of them had a knack for anything — could hardly use a hammer without hitting the wrong nail.

"This ain't changing nothing," she said, ridding herself of the tobacco cud. Reaching across the table she took Billy's cup, helped herself to a swallow of the dark bitter liquid and returned the battered tin container. "We just go right ahead doing what we schemed."

"You mean grabbing old Medford out of the jail?" Eustace asked, frowning. "That'll be hard to do, Ma, what with all that ruckus that's been kicked up over the marshal getting shot."

"We ain't taking him out of that jail," Tildy said. "You and Billy'll just lay out in that brush at the edge of town — where the road forks — and when you see which way the deputy'll be taking him, you'll up and follow 'til you come to a good place, and then you'll grab him. Like as not the deputy'll go by trail through the mountains. He'll be a mite scared of staying on the road."

"I'll be needing Pa's gun," Eustace said promptly.

Tildy gave that consideration. Then, "Yeh, I expect you will, but you behave yourself with it. Don't go shooting Case — or your brother."

"No'm, I sure won't. I been wondering about something, Ma — about Case Medford."

Tildy swiped at her stained mouth, favored her older son with a flat stare. "Can't think of nothing you got to be wondering about. Just you do what you're told."

"Yes'm, but supposing this here Case Medford'll figure, him being friends of you and Pa, that we ought to turn him loose instead of keeping him a prisoner?"

"What if he does? Don't count for nothing. Anyway, he ain't likely to see it that way. I figure us being friends of his'n, why, he'll be right glad to let us do the handing him over to the sheriff and collecting the reward instead of letting some stranger do it."

Billy, cup empty, leaned back, scratched at his tousled thatch, and wagged his head. It was a caution the way that boy was getting more and more to look like his pa. Too bad he couldn't have got a bit of Vic's sense, too.

"Eustace is right, Ma," he said. "Was I getting loose of the law I sure wouldn't be thinking to let myself be took in by no friends — I'd run."

"You ain't old enough to figure like growed folks yet," Tildy said, digging into a pocket for her twist of tobacco.

It was the last of her supply and she had

been hoarding it scrupulously, chewing it 'til there wasn't no taste left at all.

"Anyways," she continued, "being friends ain't got nothing to do with it. This here's pure damn business, and when it comes down to business, friendship ends right there."

"But, Ma," Eustace protested, perplexed, "you just said that him being a friend of yours and Pa's —"

"I know what I said," Tildy broke in sharply, "so don't go spitting it back at me. Want you both to perk up now and listen."

"Ye'm."

"Like as not it'll be that deputy — Mulky or whatever his name is . . ."

"Griff Mulky, Ma."

"All right, Griff Mulky. It'll most likely be him taking Case to Clayton City. Be real fine. Expect handling him'll be a lot easier'n it would've been if it'd been the marshal."

"Now, come first light, I want you to trot yourselves back to town. Hang around the stable or wherever the deputy keeps his horse, and find out when he'll be heading out with Case. Soon as you know, come running back here. I'll have some vittles in a sack ready for you."

"And Pa's gun," Eustace said.

"Yeh, and his gun. Then you two'll take old Jack and hightail it up to where the trail and the road forks and find yourselves a hideout."

"Then when that deputy and old Case rides by, bang, we'll grab them!" Billy said enthusiastically.

"Nope. You won't 'til you get a good chance. You'll follow them for a spell, then you'll do the grabbing," Tildy said, sternly. "And you be goddamned careful with that pistol, Eustace. I want Case alive and healthy. They maybe won't pay as much for him dead as alive. Hear?"

"Yes'm," Eustace said. Then: "You figure maybe it'd be smart was I to take Pa's gun out now and do some practice shooting? I only shot it a couple of times."

"You know how to use it without wasting no powder and lead," Tildy said. "Now, finish up your chores — and one of you trot over to the other side of the barn where we seen that woodchuck the other day. I set a snare for him. If he's caught I'll fix us up a real good stew."

"Yes'm," Eustace said, rising. "Come on, Billy. You go see about that woodchuck. I'll start chopping some wood."

"One last thing," Tildy added. "I'm expecting what you're going to do'll be done right. When I see you coming back from the hills tomorrow or next day, I sure better see Case Medford with you. If you come wagging your tail back here without him, you're going to get the hiding of your life. Hear?"

"Yes'm."

"Well, you best study on that real hard. This here's our last chance to have something, and if you boys don't do it right, we're plain up against a rock and a hard place. Like as not I'll have to go looking for saloon work again, and not being as young as I was once —"

"Don't you fret none, Ma," Billy said with full confidence. "Me and Eustace'll do it just like you want."

9

Starbuck made his way back slowly along the path that led from the Bishop house to town. He was deep in thought, having his wonder about Carla and Dave Kerry, unwilling to believe the woman could be connected with her husband's murder. But it was something he had made up his mind to look into.

Reaching the corner of the jail, Shawn halted. He might just as well have a talk with Griff Mulky now, see if he could get an inkling of what it was that Arlie Bishop wanted to tell him about Ben; he had a few questions pertaining to Bishop's death, too, that he intended to ask.

The jail was in darkness. Mulky would be inside, Shawn was certain, and he was also sure the deputy, probably a bit on the nervous side, had barred the door. He reckoned he couldn't blame Griff; if the killer, or killers, of Arlie were friends of the outlaw, Medford, and were determined to break him out of jail, they might take it in mind to try again. . . . He could talk matters over with

Griff Mulky in the morning.

Moving on to his horse, Starbuck swung onto the saddle and, turning into the street, headed down the now deserted roadway for Damson's Livery Stable. Only the saloons were alive, despite the not too late hour, and he guessed Tannekaw had not changed in that respect but still closed up early.

Gaining the livery barn, Shawn veered the sorrel into the open doorway and drew to a stop. Gus Damson, sitting at a large rolltop desk in the office he maintained just off the runway, rose immediately and came out to greet him.

"Was wondering if I'd see you again."

Starbuck came off the sorrel; pulling his rifle from its boot and hanging his saddlebags over his shoulder, he stepped back and nodded.

"Expect to be around for a day or two," he said.

A hostler came sleepily out of the shadows of the stable, took the gelding's reins, and led him off into the dim depths of the squat building, rich with the smell of fresh hay, leather, and horses.

"I'll tell him what you want," Damson said with an apologetic smile as Shawn started to call out after the elderly man. "Old Jake ain't ever but half awake this time of night. . . . You see the widow home?"

Shawn nodded, leaned against the wall of the runway. "Too bad about Arlie."

"Sure is. Was a damn good man at his job."

"Anybody come up with some idea of who it was that shot him?"

"Nope, not that I've heard of," Damson replied. "Reckon everybody's waiting for morning to do something, just what I ain't sure. You aiming to take a hand in it?"

"Arlie was my friend, but I'm not sure Henry Grissom'll take kindly to me cutting myself in on anything."

"Probably won't. Henry ain't changed all that much, and he never did have no soft spot for you after the way you stood up against him."

"Wasn't bucking him, just wanting him to let Arlie do his job without him making it double hard."

"Yeh, I know. . . . Recollect you saying back there in the jail that you'd come by to see Arlie about something."

"My brother," Shawn said, and explained the reason, concluding with: "He happen to say anything to you?"

The stableman shook his head. "Sure didn't, but Arlie was plenty close-mouthed. Never talked much to any of us in the last year or so. You ask Griff Mulky?"

"Aim to in the morning. He's got himself all buttoned up in the jail right now. No need to roust him out."

"How about Bishop's wife? You talk to her about it?"

Starbuck nodded. "Hadn't mentioned it to her, either."

Damson rubbed at the stubble on his jaw. "Well, I'm mighty sorry if it's true — about your brother being dead, I mean. You've been hunting him for quite a spell, as I recollect."

"A long time," Shawn admitted, and then pulling himself upright, he started for the doorway. "Things don't seem to have changed much around here," he continued in a casual, offhand way. "Same people except for a couple or so. This man Kerry — he a good friend of the Bishops?"

"Seems. Dave ain't been around here for too long, however. Seen him with the marshal a few times — once or twice with his missus."

"Gambler?"

"Sets in a hand at the Valley Queen now and then. Pretty fair at it, I'm told. Got plenty of money — leastwise he puts on that kind of a front."

"Mulky's a new one on me, too."

"Oh, his family's lived around here for years. They got a ranch south of here about thirty miles. Griff's all right — a mite young, but I expect he'll make it. Why? You looking for something that —"

"Just wondering who they were," Starbuck cut in, and moved on. "Guess I'll get me a room at the Far West. . . . See you in the morning."

"G'night," Damson replied, and dropped back into his office quarters.

Ignoring the friendly noise coming from the saloons, Shawn walked the short distance to the hotel and, mounting to the wide porch, crossed and entered the lobby. Two men seated in chairs, and sharing a pool of lamp-light in their reading, glanced up as he moved toward the clerk's desk. Shawn nodded slightly to each, although both were strangers, and then put his attention on Clint Albers, who rose to face him from behind the short counter.

"Sure glad to see you again, Starbuck," the hotel owner said, extending his hand. "You wanting a room?"

Shawn nodded, and propping his rifle against a nearby wall, signed the register Albers pushed at him.

"Was hoping we'd get a chance to talk before you rode out —"

Starbuck studied the man closely for a moment, then said, "Got a question or two I wanted to ask you, too." He went through the details of the message he'd received from Arlie Bishop relative to Ben.

Albers' response was the same as Gus Damson's. Bishop had not mentioned it to him, and his suggestions were along the same lines as the stableman's — talk to Griff Mulky.

"You figuring to stay around, do what you can to turn up the marshal's killer?" Albers asked then. "We can sure use somebody with your savvy."

"Don't know if I can help much, but I'm willing. Talked to Gus a bit ago. Tells me nobody's come up with any ideas of who it might be — solid ideas, I'm talking about."

"Well, for my money it was some of Medford's bunch trying to bust him out of jail. Just happened the marshal wasn't as easy to get by as they figured."

"Sounds reasonable, all right. There been any strangers show up here in the last few days?"

"Not that I've noticed. Always a few passing through that hang around awhile soaking up whiskey, then go on. Can't think of any of them that acted careful, like you'd expect."

"Probably took pains not to, if they were some of Case Medford's gang. Gus tells me the deputy's a good man. Expect he'll be able to work it all out."

Shawn was endeavoring to make his inquiries appear less direct, to avoid giving the impression that he harbored any suspicions.

"Griff? Sure, he's all right. Young and a bit hotheaded, but he'll do."

"Stranger to me — same as this friend of the Bishops, Dave Kerry."

Clint Albers' expression changed. He drew back a step and glanced around as if to be certain there were no eavesdroppers. Satisfied, he shook his head. "Him I don't put much stock in."

"Something wrong with him?"

"Plenty, far as I'm concerned. Too slick, too damned nicey-nice. Always gussied up like he was the king of some place or other and putting on a big show like he owned the world."

"He's got plenty of money, I hear."

"Who knows for sure? Always seems to, anyway."

"He a good friend of Arlie's?"

Again Albers looked about and reassured himself they were alone. "Maybe not so good as he wanted folks to think. Way I saw it, with a friend like Dave Kerry, the marshal didn't need no enemies."

Starbuck brushed his hat to the back of his head and considered that thoughtfully.

"What makes you say that?" he asked, finally.

Albers shrugged. "Maybe there was nothing for sure, but Arlie was gone a lot of the time and I always figured Kerry was hanging around Carla Bishop a bit too much."

Faint anger stirred through Starbuck. Such talk was never good, could cause the parties involved a great deal of trouble.

"But you don't know anything for sure," he said coolly.

"Nope, not anything I could put down in black and white. But it don't take much figuring. Arlie and his wife weren't getting along — and Dave Kerry was always mighty handy."

"Couldn't he be just a friend of the family's, nothing more?"

Clint Albers snorted. "When there's a fine-looking, lonesome woman like her, and a slicker like him involved? Hell's fire, Starbuck, you ain't that green!"

Shawn forced a wry grin. "Could be I am, but I make it a rule to know something like that for certain before I believe it."

Albers frowned. "Now, I never said for sure. It's only that —"

"I know what you said, and you don't need to be afraid I'll pass it on. It's their business, anyway, if there is something to it," Starbuck said, picking up the key the hotel man had laid on the desktop.

"Just how I feel about it," Albers said, his features betraying the relief he felt. "Room's at the top of the stairs to the left. You be wanting anything?"

Starbuck gripped his rifle by the barrel and wheeled for the steps leading up from the lobby. "Nothing but sleep," he said.

But he was still thinking of Clint Albers' remarks concerning Carla Bishop and Dave Kerry, adding them to what he had seen with his own eyes. A sharper, more conclusive — but not fully convincing — picture was emerging, yet he was finding it difficult to believe that Carla could have any part in Arlie's murder. Unless, of course, she, too, had changed with the years. Was such a thing possible?

10

It was a fine, spring morning. Starbuck — shaved, wearing his clean shirt, and rested from a good night's sleep — stood on the porch of the Far West Hotel and glanced along Tannekaw's main street. It was early and only a few persons were up and about — mostly merchants sweeping off their landings or the stoops that fronted their establishments, and moving merchandise out to where it could be displayed to better advantage for prospective customers.

Meadowlarks whistled in the fields that bordered the settlement, and from the corrals behind Gus Damson's livery stable a jackass brayed raucously. Two boys riding double on an aged bay gelding entered the street from the passageway lying between the marshal's office and Grissom's General Store, crossed over, and disappeared beyond Bridger's Saddle & Harness Shop. The air was warm, fragrant with the odor of lilacs in blossom — seemingly everywhere, and as yet unblemished by the smell of dust soon to be stirred into hovering layers by passing traffic.

Breakfast. . . . He hadn't enjoyed a restaurant meal in more than a week, and a man sure tired of his own cooking on the trail. Stepping down off the Far West's gallery, Starbuck angled across the roadway for the Lone Star Cafe. He raked through his mind endeavoring to recall the name of the establishment's proprietor, failed, decided as he reached the small, narrow structure that he probably had never known the owner's identity anyway. Halting at the screened door, he opened it and stepped inside.

There were no other patrons, and the burly man standing behind the counter, wearing once-white duck pants, undershirt, and a bib apron, greeted him with a disapproving frown, as if he resented the appearance of a customer at that early hour. Shawn nodded and sat down at a table next to the window.

"Bacon, eggs, fried spuds, biscuits, and coffee," he said, not waiting for the restaurant man to approach.

The order was taken in silence but almost at once the sizzle of frying meat could be heard and Shawn reckoned his needs were going to be served despite the hostile attitude of the cook.

Starbuck's thoughts dropped back to the previous night — to what he had witnessed at the Bishops' and to the insinuations Clint Albers had made concerning Dave Kerry and Carla. Again he wondered if there was some connection with Arlie's death.

The possibility disturbed him and he disliked considering it, yet there was no ignoring it. Taken at surface value, it could not be passed over; but schooled by experience in the importance of drawing no conclusions until all the facts were in, he was not accepting it.

And regardless of his personal feelings for Carla, he couldn't just walk around and forget it, even if it cost him a few days' time. Arlie Bishop had been murdered, and the fact that he had been a lawman made it doubly important that the killer — or killers — be found and brought to justice. He wasn't exactly sure how he could . . .

"You wanting honey or butter with your biscuits?"

The cook's heavy voice broke into Starbuck's thoughts and brought his attention from unseeing contemplation of the street. He looked up. The man was smiling now, friendly, congenial. He set the platter of food on the table along with a mug of coffee.

"You got a choice. Can't have both."

"Honey'll be fine," Shawn said, and picking up his knife and fork, began to eat.

The meal was good and he enjoyed it as only a healthy man could; when it was finished, he rose, paid the tab, and returned to the street.

He'd best take matters a step at a time, he decided — and the logical place to begin was with Deputy Griff Mulky at the marshal's office. Crossing over, he made his way along the gradually awakening lane to the jail.

The sound of voices rising in anger reached him as he drew near. Starbuck did not slow but continued on the board sidewalk to the front of the structure, halting finally at the thick, iron-bound door, still closed. Grasping the latch, he tried the heavy panel. It did not budge. The crossbar inside was still in its brackets.

"What do you want?" Mulky's voice demanded irritably.

Starbuck's jaw hardened at the man's offensive tone. "Open up, Deputy," he answered coldly.

A few moments of silence followed, and then the scrape of the bar being lifted, the thud as it was set aside, reached Shawn. The door swung back with a jerk and Mulky framed himself in the opening, blocking it.

"What do you want?" he repeated.

"To do some talking," Shawn said curtly, and stepping up into the building's entrance, he shouldered his way by the young lawman into the room. "Name's Starbuck."

"I know who you are," the deputy snapped, wheeling.

Shawn halted in front of a second man, a slim, dark individual with narrow features. "Name's Starbuck," he said again, extending his hand to force the introduction.

The man, wearing worn, faded range clothing, bobbed. "Glad to know you. I'm Jim Docket. Folks call me Jig."

"You don't have to tell him nothing," Mulky cut in angrily. "He ain't nothing around here — was a friend of the marshal's, that's all, and he's just riding through."

"In a couple of days, maybe," Starbuck corrected in a quiet voice. "First want to talk to you about Bishop."

"I ain't got nothing to say that I ain't already said."

"Could be. This is something else. What I want to ask concerns my brother, Ben."

"Ain't never heard of him," Mulky snapped, and moving to the chair behind the desk, sat down.

Keeping a tight rein on his temper, Shawn turned to where he could face the young lawman.

"Bishop sent word to me that he knew something about Ben. I've been trying to find him for some time. The message said that he was dead or maybe only had been shot. I don't know for sure what the story is. That's what brought me here, but the marshal was killed before I got a chance to see him."

"So —"

Docket had drifted over to one of the benches placed against the wall and had settled onto it. Back in the room where the cells were built, Medford was rattling the cage's door insistently.

"He mention to you what it was all about?"

"Never said nothing to me," Mulky stated flatly. "But that ain't special. Never was one to tell me anything. Kept everything to hisself like he was scared he might say something that'd cost him a dollar or two."

Starbuck considered the deputy thoughtfully. "I take it you didn't much like the marshal —"

"I hated his guts," Mulky replied in a calm, decisive way, "and whoever the hell it was that plugged him done me a mighty good turn."

"Why?" Shawn asked, continuing to study the man.

"Gets him out of my way, that's why. Job now'll be mine, and it'll be me collecting them big rewards instead of him hogging it all."

"Gives you a good reason to kill him."

Mulky laughed. "Sure does, don't it? Only it wasn't."

"You prove it?"

The deputy scratched at the sparse field of whiskers on his jaw. "Who says I got to?" he demanded, evasively.

"Probably be quite a few people around town who'd be expecting you to."

"Let them expect," Mulky said indifferently. "They can't prove nothing against me."

"It'll be your problem," Starbuck said. Then, "I understand you and Bishop had words over the bounty being paid for Case Medford?"

"We sure'n hell did — a'plenty of them! Part of that reward's mine and he damn well knew it, but he plain out told me to forget it. Was all his, he claimed."

"Was him that caught Medford, wasn't it?"

"Reckon so, but it was me staying here doing his job for him while he was off running Case down. I figure that makes him owe me and I've got a chunk of that five thousand coming."

Starbuck shrugged. "Feeling the way you did about Bishop, you'd better have some proof that it couldn't have been you that shot him down. . . . What're you going to do about the killer — if it wasn't you?"

"What the hell can I do? Took a look around last night, didn't turn up nothing."

"You leaving it at that?"

Griff Mulky shifted on his chair. "I got plenty of other things to do right now — like getting Medford to Clayton City."

"Longer you wait before starting to do your looking around, the colder the trail will be. You ought to be out asking questions. There's a good chance somebody got at least a glimpse of the killer."

"Was nobody spoke up last night saying they did."

"That's no proof there wasn't. Folks living close by could've seen whoever it was leaving here — running, maybe — and didn't give it any thought, specially if they weren't in that crowd gathered in the street last night."

Mulky stirred restlessly again. "Aim to do some investigating," he muttered. "Sure don't need you or nobody else telling me how to do my job —"

Starbuck smiled coolly. "I'd say you need something," he said, and turned to face the doorway at the sound of a light footstep.

A small, sober-eyed girl in a shoe-top length calico dress entered the room hesitantly. She glanced about, settled her attention on Shawn. He didn't need to be told this was Jeannie Bishop; the child was the image of her mother.

"Are you Mr. Starbuck?" she asked.

Shawn nodded. "What can I do for you, Jeannie?"

The girl's diffidence vanished at mention of her name. "Mama wants you to come to our house for breakfast," she said with a smile.

Starbuck gave that brief thought. He'd already had his meal but it was possible that Carla had remembered something she felt was important and wanted to talk to him. He could settle for coffee.

"It'll be a real pleasure, young lady," he said, and crossing the room, took her by the hand and moved toward the door. Reaching there, he glanced over his shoulder to the deputy.

"I'll be back," he said. "Like to go through that desk, see if there's a note or something that'll tell me what the marshal wanted to see me about."

Mulky shook his head. "There ain't nothing —"

"How do you know?" Starbuck pressed, pausing on the step.

"Maybe I don't, exactly, but I'm the marshal here now, and I ain't about to let every drifter that comes through here go pawing around in my things."

"Up to you, but I reckon I can get the mayor's permission if I need it," Starbuck said, shrugging, and continued on with Jeannie Bishop.

11

"My papa died," Jeannie said as they started up the path to the Bishop house. She spoke with the matter-of-fact blandness of a child not yet having reached the age of total comprehension.

"I'm sorry to hear that," Starbuck replied. "He was a fine man."

The girl's small, round face flushed with pleasure. "Were you his friend?"

"Yes, I met him and your mama a long time ago. You weren't much more than a baby."

"I don't remember you," Jeannie said, frankly.

Shawn grinned. Leave it to children to be bluntly honest! Undoubtedly he could ask the youngster a few questions concerning the relationship of her mother with Dave Kerry and get true answers, but he was not about to stoop to taking such advantage.

"Here's my house," Jeannie announced suddenly, and pulling free of Starbuck's hand, she ran on ahead, calling to her mother as she did.

Shawn followed the child into the yard, aware again of the overriding perfume of the lilacs growing around the place, and halted at the edge of the porch as Carla stepped into view.

In a dress of dark blue, her hair pulled to the back of her head where she had fastened it into a bun, she was serene and lovely in the early light.

"Thank you for coming, Shawn," she said, greeting him soberly, and then handing a small pail to Jeannie, added, "Here's your lunch, dear. Run on to school now."

The youngster took the tin and, smiling widely at Starbuck, said goodbye and hurried off in the direction of town.

"I've told her about Arlie," Carla said, holding the door open for Starbuck, "but she doesn't really understand."

"Can see that. Too young —"

"It's only partly that," Carla said, turning back into the house. "He's been gone so much these past years that she hardly knew him. . . . Do you mind eating in the kitchen? It's so much nicer in there."

"Suits me fine — and I've already had my meal. Can use a cup of coffee, however."

Following Carla through the house, noting absently the door through which he had seen Kerry enter, Shawn gave her words concerning Arlie Bishop's absence deeper thought.

"Never realized that he was away all that much."

"It wasn't that he was out of town, he just hardly ever came home," Carla said, filling cups for Shawn and herself as he settled onto a chair. "Truth is, there was another woman."

Starbuck voiced no comment as she sat down on the opposite side of the table. That the subject was painful to her was to be expected, and he had no wish to pry into the matter. He wondered then — if what he suspected concerning her friendship with Dave Kerry was true — which came first, Bishop's other woman, or the tall, handsome Kerry? Which brought on the other?

"But that doesn't matter now," Carla went on. "It stopped hurting a long time ago. My big worry is that Arlie spent a lot of the money he made on her, besides losing quite a bit gambling. I have very little left of what I was able to get from him for us to live on — and there's Jeannie to raise."

Starbuck took a swallow of coffee. He was learning more and more about Arlie Bishop — certainly not the man he'd known.

"I'd like to help," he began but Carla waved him into silence.

"Thank you — I'm too proud for charity, especially from you. It won't be necessary, anyway, if you'll do me a favor — a big one."

"Name it."

"Case Medford. Deliver him to the sheriff in Clayton City and collect the reward money for me."

Starbuck nodded. "Sure, but won't the deputy, or somebody picked by Henry Grissom, be doing that?"

"That's probably the plan, but I don't trust any of them, Griff Mulky least of all. The way he felt about Arlie I know he'll —"

"Can understand how you feel about him. We had a little talk this morning."

"Then you can see why I'm asking this of you, Shawn. We talked it over last night and —"

"We?"

"Dave Kerry and me. He dropped by not long after you left."

Starbuck felt a measure of relief slip through him. "Yeh, I saw him."

Carla leaned forward, studied him closely, her eyes puzzled, curious. A faint smile parted her lips.

"Surely you don't think that Dave and I — that we've been, well, carrying on?"

Blunt, Starbuck said, "Had the look of it — him showing up late, hanging around in the bushes for a while like he wanted to be sure nobody was watching."

"He was making certain there was nobody else here, all right, but not for the reason you think. Dave had an idea that whoever it was that killed Arlie might try to harm Jeannie and me."

Such was an acceptable explanation for Kerry's actions but it mattered little to Starbuck now; what was important was that Carla had voluntarily admitted Dave Kerry's visit in a frank and open manner — and that, so far as he was concerned, removed them from being suspect.

"I assure you, Shawn, Dave's only a friend — a good one. Oh, I won't say he wouldn't like to be more, but it's all on his part — none of it on mine."

"How'd Arlie feel about him?"

"He didn't like Dave much. I guess he suspected how Dave felt about me, and maybe he was a little jealous even though he was anything but a good husband himself."

"They ever have words?"

"Not that I know of. Arlie got angry at him two or three times, but I think it was over something else, gambling, perhaps. . . . Shawn, I don't want you to hold anything against Dave Kerry. He's only trying to help me. It was him, in fact, that came up with the suggestion that I ask you to take Medford to Clayton City?"

"Why would he do that? Man doesn't know me — saw me for the first time last night at the jail."

"He knows you're a good friend of Arlie's and mine, and that we both trust you."

"A bit surprised he didn't offer to do the job himself."

"I think Dave realizes he'd not be the man for the job. There could be trouble — I hope you realized that before you agreed."

"Hadn't given it any thought, but if Medford's gang is hanging around, along with a scatter of bounty hunters, there could be plenty."

Alarm lifted in Carla Bishop's eyes. "Will that make a difference to you?"

"No, changes nothing."

Carla settled back. "I was thinking that if it did, you could get some men, hire them to ride along with you like a posse, or escort."

"One way, all right. Trouble is, that would draw plenty of attention, and if there is a bunch going to make a try for Medford, we'd have a regular shootout. Best to avoid that if we can. Smart thing will be to go it alone, slip off with him if I can without anybody knowing about it. Easy for just two riders to move without being seen if they take pains. Hard to hide a whole posse."

"Of course. Dave said he was sure you'd

know best. . . . That money means so much to me, Shawn. Just about everything — Jeannie's future and mine."

"You taking it and going back to New York?"

"No, we'll stay here. Mrs. Purdy — she owns the women's and children's store — wants to sell out. She's getting along in years. With the reward money, I can buy her out and have a means of support for Jeannie and me. There'd even be quite a bit of cash left over to fall back on — in the event business didn't do well at the start."

"Sounds like a good plan," Starbuck said. "You intend to talk this over with the mayor and Griff Mulky?"

"Having you take charge of Case Medford, you mean? I don't think it's necessary, but Dave said he'd talk to Henry Grissom if need be — and I have a few friends who'll stand by me. I don't think there's anyone that will dispute my claim to the reward. As for Griff Mulky, I don't care whether he likes the idea or not."

"Heard Grissom say last night that he didn't want the deputy leaving town. That should settle it."

Carla's slim shoulders stirred indifferently. "He'll do what he's told. After all, it was Arlie who caught Medford, and he's already notified the sheriff in Clayton City that he'd be bringing Medford in and to have the money ready. When will you leave?"

Carla Bishop was convinced there'd be no problem with Deputy Griff Mulky, and perhaps there wouldn't be. But Henry Grissom was no friend of his, Starbuck was recalling, and the mayor himself just might prove to be the stumbling block in her plans. He'd not mention it or worry her with the possibility, however. Let it develop — and then handle it.

"As soon get it done," he replied. "When is Arlie's funeral?"

"This afternoon. Why?"

"Expect most of the town will be there. I'm thinking that would be a good time to head out with Medford. We could be a long way from here before folks knew we had gone. Don't like the idea of not going to the funeral, though. Arlie was my friend. I ought to be there."

"He'd understand why you're not. What you're doing is for him — and for Jeannie and me."

"That's how I'll have to look at it," Starbuck said, rising. "Think now I'll get back to the jail, start lining up things."

Carla got to her feet, trailed him to the front door. "Do you want me to have Dave talk to Mayor Grissom?"

He shook his head and, stepping out onto the porch, set his hat in place. "Leave it to me. I'll tell the deputy, and we'll go from there."

Carla nodded, a soft smile on her lips. "Thank you, Shawn. This means so much to me — and your being here has set my mind at ease. I won't worry about anything now."

Starbuck's features sobered. "Nothing's for sure in this world," he warned. "We'll hope that if anybody tries taking Case Medford away from me, I'll be able to stop him."

"You will," Carla said confidently.

12

Jig Docket was in the marshal's office again when Starbuck entered, but whatever problem existed between him and Deputy Mulky had apparently been resolved, as the two men now were on the best of terms.

As Shawn stepped through the doorway, Docket at once wheeled, nodded in smiling, friendly fashion, said, " 'Morning," and hurriedly took his leave, moving off at a peculiar, hitching gait.

"Got something on that killer," Mulky said before Starbuck could speak. "Jig found this here slicker out back of the jail in some weeds. I'm betting he was wearing it."

Shawn nodded. Mulky's attitude toward him had somehow undergone a change, too, it seemed. "That's a start. Any idea who it belongs to?"

"Nope, not yet. Ain't no markings on it, but I aim to do plenty of asking around."

"If the killer was wearing it, there's a good chance he stole it, used it during the shooting, and then threw it away."

"Figured that, too," Mulky said promptly. "Still, gives me something to work on. If it's somebody else's property, maybe they'll recollect who it was that could've stole it."

"You're on the right track," Starbuck said, and glanced toward the door, presently closed, that led into the room where the cells were built. "Mind if I have a look at your prisoner?"

Shawn, ordinarily direct in his methods, was working gradually to the point of telling the deputy of Carla Bishop's desire to have him escort Case Medford to Clayton City. That it clearly was the deputy's job had to be admitted, and he doubted the man would relinquish the chore unless compelled to do so; handing over an outlaw as notorious as Medford to the higher authorities would up Mulky's status as a lawman considerably, so objection was to be expected. Of course Henry Grissom could overrule the deputy, but Starbuck hoped it would not come down to bringing the mayor in on the matter.

Moving to the door, he pulled it open, and walked into the hall-like area. Case Medford, eating his morning meal, glanced up. Somewhere in his forties, he was a dark, stocky man with thick shoulders, a square jaw, and overhanging brows that shaded deepset, small, black eyes. He met Shawn's gaze with a surly grin.

"Who the hell are you?"

"No friend of yours," Starbuck answered shortly, and pulling back, he returned to the office.

"He's a hard one," Mulky said, with a shake of his head. "They're wanting him for a couple of murders along with a half of dozen holdups and robberies. Reason there's such a big bounty on him."

"It all right with you if I'm the one to take him to Clayton City?"

Mulky, sitting at his desk sorting through a sheaf of papers, paused, then shrugged. "Sure. Makes no difference to me."

Surprise rolled through Starbuck. He had expected instant opposition, but Mulky appeared pleased.

"The marshal's wife — widow — asked me to do it as a favor to her."

"Kind of figured she would, you being a big friend of hers — and his," the young lawman said. "And you're sure welcome to the job." Hesitating, he opened a drawer in the desk, procured a deputy's badge, and tossed it to Shawn. "Reckon you best wear this. I'm swearing you in here and now."

Starbuck dropped the star into his shirt pocket. What Mulky was doing probably was illegal, but carrying a badge was a good idea.

"When you figure to head out with him?"

Shawn glanced toward the street. He wasn't certain how far he could trust the deputy, and the man's lack of resistance to his taking charge of the prisoner bothered him. He had not forgotten Mulky's claim that he should share in the reward being paid for Case Medford, and his open hostility concerning Arlie Bishop.

"Today, maybe tonight," he said. "Like to slip off without folks noticing."

"Smart thing to do," Griff agreed readily. "If he's got his bunch hanging around waiting, you'd best try and leave without them seeing you. Anything you want me to do?"

"I'll be needing whatever papers you've got that have to be turned over to the sheriff in Clayton City."

"His name's Saffire — John Saffire."

"And if you'll have Medford's horse out back and him ready to go —"

"Sure. Can do that easy without drawing much attention. There's a shed behind the jail. I'll put his horse in it. How soon'll you be wanting this done?"

"Right away. I figure to pull out when things look right. Could be an hour from now, or maybe it'll be after dark."

Mulky nodded. "I savvy. How about some grub? It's about a four-day ride."

"Got a bit in my saddlebags but I'll need more with him to feed."

"I'll see to that, too," Mulky said, coming to his feet. "Want you to know I'm obliged to you, Starbuck. Takes a load off my mind — getting rid of Medford. I'll leave a pair of irons and the keys here on top of my desk along with the papers if it happens I ain't around when you take the notion to pull out."

Deputy Griff Mulky was going out of his way to be cooperative, Shawn thought, and he knew that he should appreciate it — and he did. But the turnabout in the lawman's attitude disturbed him.

"Be obliged to you," he said, moving for the door. "Like to keep all this between us two."

Mulky was close on his heels. "Sure, I understand. Getting Medford off my back'll let me get busy at digging up the marshal's killer, like I'm supposed to be doing," he said cheerfully as they stepped out into the street. "Be seeing you later."

Starbuck watched the lawman hurry off in the direction of the general store, apparently to lay in the supply of trail grub he figured would be necessary. Henry Grissom would now be aware of the arrangements made, and if Tannekaw's mayor was going to raise any objections they would come soon, but here again Shawn determined to face that problem if and when it faced him.

Wheeling, he bent his steps for Damson's livery barn, reaching there just as Gus was coming up from the rear of the building where he had been performing some chore.

"You after your sorrel?" the stableman asked.

Starbuck bobbed. "Expect to be using him some time today. Like for you to have him saddled and put in that shed behind the jail."

"Sure thing," Damson said, and then frowned. "You pulling out?"

Shawn was certain he could trust Gus Damson, although he had earlier decided to keep the number of persons in on his plans as few as possible. But there was no excluding the stableman; he needed his advice as to the route he would follow.

"Don't say anything about this," he said, "but I'm the one taking Medford to Clayton City."

The stableman's brows came up in surprise. "You?"

"Carla Bishop asked me to do it as a favor. She seems a little scared it might not turn out right for her if somebody else did the job."

"Probably right. What's the deputy think about it?"

"He's all for it. Hardly expected that after the way he unloaded on me about Arlie and how he ought to be sharing in the reward. Being real helpful in getting things set for me to go."

Damson wagged his head doubtfully. "Folks always say a man hadn't ought to look a gift horse in the mouth, but Griff Mulky being helpful — I just don't know."

"I'm not putting too much trust in him," Shawn said, "or anybody else outside of you and Carla Bishop. And Dave Kerry. He was in on it from the start."

"I see. When'll you be leaving?"

"Haven't decided exactly. Be some time today. I wanted to ask you about getting there — Clayton City."

"Only two ways I know of — the main road and the old trail through the mountains. Of course a man could forget both, cut straight across through the hills, but it'd take him twice as long."

"What's the trail like?"

"Never was real good — that's the main reason folks quit using it. Man riding horseback'll find it kind of hard going, wagon'd never get through at all. You'll make better time on the road."

"I'm more interested in just making it through."

Damson turned his head, spat. "Yeh, I know what you mean. There anything for certain that Medford's gang is hanging around?"

"Not that I've heard, but I'm taking no chances. It's not only important that I get Medford to Clayton City and collect the bounty for Carla Bishop, but that I come out of it with a whole skin, too."

"Can't fault you there. Was I you, I'd take him by the trail. Odds are somebody wanting to stop you'll be along the road. You'll find plenty of cover on the trail. You know how to get on it?"

"No, haven't been up that way."

"Just head north out of town. When you come to the foot of the mountain there'll be a fork. Trail cuts off to the left, road'll keep going to the right. . . . You find out anything about your brother?"

"Haven't had a chance to go through Arlie's papers yet," Shawn said. As on so many previous occasions, his own needs and interests would have to be pushed aside, wait until he had time to attend them. "Aim to get busy at it soon as I'm back."

Gus Damson smiled tightly. "Just you be damn sure you get back, hear?"

"Figure to do my best," Starbuck replied, and swung back into the street.

He'd best go see Carla, tell her everything was arranged — and caution her to say nothing about it. That she and Dave Kerry could be trusted with his plans was unquestionable, but counting them, there were now four — five if Henry Grissom had been told — who knew he would be heading north with Case Medford shortly. He still held the trump card, however; none of them knew exactly when.

13

The midafternoon sun had turned hot. Starbuck, astride his sorrel, with Case Medford, cuffed and loosely roped on a bay a length ahead, looked back as they slowly ascended the mountain trail.

"Pull up," he called.

The outlaw halted, swung half around. "What do you want?"

Shawn ignored the question, his attention fixed on the slope just west of the now distant settlement. Arlie Bishop's funeral was coming to a close. He could see but not make out definitely the people gathered there and that were now beginning to disperse. He would have liked to attend the services. Arlie had been a friend, one who had tried to do him a favor by sending word regarding Ben, and he felt he owed it to the lawman to pay his last respects.

But by the same measure he owed Arlie Bishop's widow, and he could best demonstrate his friendship by doing as she had asked and making certain she received the reward the lawman was due.

"That the marshal they're planting?" Medford asked in his deep, heavy voice.

Shawn nodded.

"Expect you'll be the next one the preacher'll be saying words over."

"Maybe," Starbuck replied, uninterestedly.

A buggy was pulling away from the fairly large crowd that had assembled. In it would be Carla and her small daughter — and most likely Dave Kerry, Shawn guessed.

"Ain't no maybe to it," Medford continued. "I got friends waiting for me up the line. You ain't never going to get me to no hanging tree in Clayton City."

"Seems to me they're not having much luck helping you," Shawn said, now prying for information. "They tried last night, didn't make it. Be the same next time."

"That wasn't them," the outlaw said. "Don't know who it was, and I sure don't give a damn — just adds up to there being one less badge-toter. Like as not it was some jasper looking to square up a raw deal with that marshal."

"Or maybe a bounty hunter hoping to collect on your scalp," Starbuck commented dryly.

The outlaw grunted, spat. "Yep, it could've been — only he'd sure be wasting his time.

My boy'll look after me. I reckon they're setting back up the mountain a piece watching us right now — and waiting. You taking this old trail instead of the road ain't going to fool them none."

"Don't bet on it."

"And riding at night won't make no difference, either. I've been seeing that big moon you're banking on. It'll make it easy for them to see, same as it will you."

"Works for the bounty hunters, too," Starbuck said.

The crowd had all but deserted the cemetery on the hillside, only the sexton remaining now to do the final chores. Carla would be returning to her home, where she would await his coming, convinced that he would be able to carry out his mission successfully and at no danger to himself. He wished he could be as certain.

"You figure there's some bounty hunters looking for me?" Medford asked, a thread of doubt now running through his tone.

"Why not?" Shawn answered in an offhand way. "With a reward big as you've got on your head, there's bound to be. That's what got you caught, wasn't it?"

"Yeh, that goddam little two-bit marshal. Tricked me. But I ain't faulting him for it. Was his job and I was a dumb fool to let him grab me. You one of his deputies? Don't recollect seeing you around 'til this morning."

"I've got a star," Shawn answered, and touched the badge in his shirt pocket.

The mourners, or at least those who had attended Arlie Bishop's last rites, were now gone from view. Starbuck turned back and glanced ahead to the narrowly defined path lifting before them to the mountain's first ridge.

"You worrying some, Deputy?" Medford said in a bantering voice.

"No, just having a look at what's in front of us."

"Yeh, that'll do to tell. You're doing some curling inside right about now, and your guts're starting to kick up. If you ain't a plain fool wanting to commit suicide, you'll be thinking about what you're trying to do."

"What's there to think about? I'm taking you to Clayton City, turning you over to a sheriff named John Saffire. That's all there is to it."

"All!" Case Medford shouted with a laugh. "Mister Deputy, that ain't the half of it! Smartest thing you can do is take these irons off me and turn me loose."

Shawn grinned. "Sounds to me like you're not so sure your friends'll be waiting to help you."

"The hell! It sure ain't that. I'm just trying to save your neck for you. My boys are kind of mean when it comes to badge-toters, and if they ever start in on you, folks'll find it a mighty hard chore to figure out just who it is they're burying."

"Plenty tough, that it?"

"Can chaw that twice and more! Now, you seem like a real smart man, Deputy —"

"Name's Starbuck."

"All right, Starbuck. Like I said, you seem like a smart kind of fellow. Why'n't we make us a deal —"

"Move out, Medford," Shawn cut in, having allowed the outlaw to run on long enough. "You're just wasting breath — and you better save all you got while you can. It's going to run out of you fast when they put that rope around your neck in Clayton City."

Case Medford swore. "Won't never happen, friend," he said tightly. "I'm guaranteeing you that — same as I'll guarantee you that you won't even get me to Clayton City."

"Going to be plenty of folks disappointed, including me, if I don't," Shawn said, and motioned at the outlaw to do as he'd been directed.

Medford cut his bay about, started on up the grade fairly steep at that point. After a few minutes he looked back.

"You a gambling man, Deputy? You want to make a little bet?"

"Not interested."

"No? Well, I just wanted to lay you big odds that you'll never see that hunter's moon you're banking on traveling by tonight. That's what you've got in mind, ain't it?"

Starbuck let the question ride.

"Them friends of mine are 'way ahead of you. That big old moon's going to be shining down on us and showing them right where we are — that is, if they let you keep going 'til it comes out. Telling you again, you best start thinking about the deal I'm willing to offer. You turn me loose right now and I won't let them work you over."

Shawn closed his ears to the outlaw's continual haranguing. What Medford said, of course, could be true; his friends — his boys as he liked to call them — probably were somewhere on the mountain, or would be eventually. There was a good chance they had posted themselves along the main road, had by that hour discovered he had instead taken the trail, and were hastening to correct their error if they had not already done so.

All of which hinged on whether Medford was telling the truth or not in claiming that he had friends waiting to help him. That was the question; the outlaw had made it clear that it was not his men who had killed Arlie Bishop in an effort to free him, and that could lead to the belief that Medford had no allies in the area.

But such was only a possibility and Starbuck knew he could not accept it as a fact — or even as something to be hoped for. He could only play it safe and assume the outlaw had followers and that somewhere along the way they would make their move to take Medford from him.

The same held true where bounty hunters were concerned, although he doubted, as someone had suggested, that it was one such man, or several, coveting the big reward offered for Medford, who had killed Arlie Bishop. It wasn't logical to believe that anyone would walk into a jail in the center of a settlement, shoot down the marshal, and attempt to take a prisoner from a cell.

That was not to say, however, that there wouldn't be bounty hunters waiting, as Medford claimed his friends would be, in ambush along the route to Clayton City. He knew he must be on the alert for them just as much as he should be for friends of Case Medford.

Who, then, had killed Arlie Bishop?

Starbuck's thoughts shifted to that question as his eyes moved back and forth over the surrounding country. The slope up which they were traveling was mostly covered with rock, had only small clumps of oak and similar brush growing on its surface, and offered little in the way of cover for an ambush. Anyone with such a plan in mind would seek more suitable terrain.

If it wasn't any of Medford outlaw crowd, and if it wasn't a bounty hunter, who then had it been? He hadn't been afforded the time to inquire into Bishop's activities or to search about for enemies who might take it on themselves to settle a grudge with a bullet, so he was at a loss there. Carla had said Arlie was gambling, evidently for considerable amounts. Also, she had mentioned another woman in the picture. Both factors offered possibilities.

And there was Griff Mulky, who spared nothing in making it clear how he felt about the lawman and who, unaccountably, had undergone a sudden change in attitude. When he thought about it, Shawn realized the deputy had plenty to gain by Arlie's death.

"Starbuck —"

Shawn put his attention on the outlaw. "Yeh?"

"You figure to pull up and do some eating? Never had no chance to eat my dinner."

Starbuck glanced at the sun, now well on its path to the horizon in the west, then pointed to a towering, rocky hogback a good hour's ride in the distance.

"Can stop there and eat while we wait for dark. Be moving on when the moon comes up."

"Won't do you no good. My boys'll still spot us."

"Works both ways," Shawn said, and resumed his steady, scouring vigilance of the hillside.

14

Starbuck halted in a grassless little hollow behind the hogback. The sun had dropped behind the ragged skyline to the west and an amber glow, fading rapidly, had spread over the hills.

Dismounting, he secured the big sorrel to a scrub oak and then, stepping up to Case Medford, helped him from the saddle — after which he picketed the outlaw's horse alongside his own.

Medford raised his manacled arms. "Don't reckon there's any use of me asking you to take these goddam irons off'n me. I'll give you my word —"

"Forget it," Starbuck cut in and pointed to a flat rock half buried near the palisade-like wall of the ridge. "Set there while I get together something to eat."

Medford muttered under his breath, but under Starbuck's steady, unrelenting gaze, he crossed the swale and settled on the rock.

Shawn, rummaging about in the sack of food Griff Mulky had provided, and digging out from his saddlebags the tin he used for making coffee along with a frying pan, selected a spot fanned by the slight breeze that had sprung to life at sundown and built a fire.

He used dry sticks blown in under the overhang since they would create a minimum of smoke, but this was more or less instinctive, for he gave little thought to it. Darkness would shortly blanket the hills, at least until moonrise, and the chances of the fire drawing attention were small.

"We camping here tonight?" Medford asked.

Starbuck did not reply. The outlaw knew his plan was to ride on once it was light enough to follow the trail; evidently Case had in mind nothing more than idle conversation and he was in no mood for such.

He continued with the meal preparation — no more than dried beef chunked into the spider with water and a can of tomatoes added, heated to a boil and served on thick chunks of bread as a stew, to be washed down with strong, black coffee.

"You ain't talking, that it?"

Starbuck, deeming the concoction in the pan had cooked sufficiently, spooned a quantity onto a tin plate and passed it to the outlaw.

"We'll be moving out soon's the moon's

up," he said, more to close the man off than impart information. Filling a cup with coffee from the lard tin, he placed it on the rock beside the outlaw and returned to the opposite side of the hollow.

"Still ain't too late to change your mind about turning me loose," Medford said, his cheeks bulging with an over-large mouthful of stew.

Shawn, eating slowly, was listening into the rising darkness. The lower areas were already clothed in shadows and the blackness was creeping steadily up the slopes, claiming the rocks, the brush, and the trees. Overhead the sky was still a softly glowing canopy of pearl from which the more vivid hues of color had all but faded.

"Expect my boys are moving in on you right now. Smart thing'll be for us to make a deal before they show up. Ain't sure I can make them mind once they get here and see me with these irons on my wrists."

Shawn, hunger satisfied, threw the remainder of the stew onto the leaf-littered ground for the birds and small varmints to feast upon, and refilling his cup with coffee, rose to his feet to have a look at the surrounding country.

Medford laughed. "Getting a mite jumpy, Deputy? Sure don't blame you, 'cause you ain't got the chance of a grasshopper in a chicken yard of ever getting out of these hills alive unless you listen to me. Now, I —"

Starbuck half turned and looked down at the outlaw. In the dying light, his strong, rugged features took on a dark, bronzed look and his eyes appeared flint-hard in their deep recesses. Medford's words broke off abruptly, something in the tall man's manner warning him to silence.

Shawn continued to stare at the outlaw, his mind filled with no particular thought other than that of possibly gagging the man as a means of eliminating the constant yammering in which he had not the slightest interest.

After a time he came back around, threw his attention back along the slope up which they had come. He had heard, or thought he had, the faint click of metal against stone — the sound that an approaching horse might make. He listened intently. From somewhere nearby a bird chirped sleepily, and over on a distant slope the first coyote barked a welcome to the coming night — but that was all. There was no repeat of the metallic click.

Starbuck shifted his glance to the eastern horizon. Complete darkness had taken over and now a bright flare marked the imminent moon. . . . If it was a horse he'd heard, there was little doubt it would be either Medford's friends or a bounty hunter; it was unlikely anyone else would be on the trail at that hour.

"You hearing something, Deputy?" Case Medford called in a mocking voice through the half dark. "Expect it's my boys a'coming."

Again ignoring the outlaw, Starbuck dropped back to the center of the hollow, collecting the utensils they had used, he stowed them in his saddlebags, beckoned to Medford, and jerked a thumb toward the horses.

"Mount up —"

Medford pulled himself erect, swaggered across the swale. "You getting anxious, Deputy? Seems I recollect you saying we'd wait for the moon."

Shawn waited until the outlaw was in the saddle and then replaced the rope about his waist. Drawing the loop snug, he freed the reins of the two horses and went onto the sorrel. Wheeling, he faced Medford squarely.

"Want you to know this," he said in a cold, matter-of-fact voice. "You let out one yell and I'll drag you off that horse and take you up the trail the hard way. Going to be up to you."

Medford was silent for a long breath. Finally he shrugged. "You're a mighty tough customer, Deputy — and a plenty dumb one. You'll be changing your tune when my boys catch up with us."

"I doubt they will," Shawn replied laconically, and cutting the gelding about, he gestured toward the ragged path, barely visible in the poor light. "Let's go."

They moved out, and then shortly the moon broke over the rim in the east and began to flood the country with its yellow glow. More coyotes took up the challenge and the stillness echoed eerily with their discordant yapping.

The trail now lay clearly visible in the night, winding through the rocks and the brush and smaller trees as it climbed gradually into higher levels where the pines and firs would predominate.

If they were being followed, Starbuck reasoned, he would be to better advantage among those larger trees where they would be less noticeable. He had no plan in mind other than to avoid a showdown with Medford's outlaw gang, number unknown, or any bounty hunters, also of undetermined quantity — and, if it became necessary, to make a stand in the best possible place and shoot it out.

It could be that he had not actually heard the snick of a horseshoe against rock, that Medford had no friends planning to rescue him from the rope, and that there were no bounty hunters in the offing. There had been no actual indication of such in Tannekaw, only assumptions, but Shawn took no solace from that; he could only prepare himself for such an eventuality should it develop.

That was the hardest part of facing up to danger, Starbuck had long ago discovered — the not knowing if there actually was danger. It was far easier to cope if a man was aware of what he was up against; it was the unknown that made it difficult and even possibly disastrous.

They topped out a ridge and started across a bald saddle. Shawn turned, glanced back. His jaw tightened. Far below on the trail, clearly silhouetted in the now bright moonlight, were three riders. He watched them briefly, and stiffened as he saw further movement off on a side slope to their left — a single horse moving slowly through the shadows.

He came back around, gave that consideration. Four in the party, with one member, for some unexplainable reason, skirting the main trail that was being taken by the others.

"Deputy —"

Medford's grating voice reached back to him. The outlaw was not yet conscious of his friends' presence.

"How long we going to keep riding? I'm getting mighty tired of setting on this saddle."

"You'll live," Starbuck replied curtly.

But the outlaw's question had given him an idea. The main road connecting Clayton City with Tannekaw lay to the east, on the far side of the mountains looming up to their right. It shouldn't be too hard to swing away from the trail at the first convenient opportunity, cross over, and rejoin the road. With luck the outlaws would continue along the path in the belief Medford and his captor were still ahead of them.

The principal risk was the possibility of their being seen while they were crossing over, he realized as he studied the slope stretching out to meet the summit of the mountain. Trees were sparse because of the nearness of timberline, and the ground, in the silvered light, looked to be covered with grass and low-growing shrubs and weeds.

It would be wiser to draw off to the side, find a place to hole up, and allow the outlaws to bypass them. When they were far enough along the trail to become indistinct, then would be the time to make the change and head for the road.

Starbuck raised himself in the stirrups and glanced over to a blufflike formation in the near distance to the left. It was marked with deep shadows indicating many clefts and gullies. It should offer any number of effective places in which to lay over for the necessary length of time.

Raking the sorrel gelding lightly with his

spurs, Shawn moved up beside Medford. It would still be best not to let the outlaw know that his followers were in the vicinity; he might take it upon himself to yell in the hope of drawing their attention, despite the threat of what would happen to him if he did so.

"Horses are getting tired," he said, scanning the trail before them. "We'll have to pull over and rest for a bit."

"Was what I was saying," the outlaw grumbled.

Starbuck pointed to the formation. "There's a draw up ahead that'll take us to those bluffs. Swing into it."

Medford straightened in protest. "What the hell's the use of going that far? Why can't we just haul up along here somewheres?"

"Old rule of mine," Shawn said dryly. "Don't ever sleep on the trail. Could wake up and find you've got company. Move on."

15

Red Rockmond, shifting his weight on the saddle, swore wearily. "When the hell you reckon that goddam lawman's going to pull up for the night?"

From behind him Dow sighed. "Had him figured to stop back there on the ridge."

The red-haired outlaw stirred again on the leather. He glanced over his shoulder. Abe Ladner, bringing up the rear of the brief procession, was sleeping, rocking gently back and forth with the motion of his horse. It was to be expected; Abe had spent the previous night and most of the morning shacked up with a saloon girl — Gypsy, he thought she was called.

It was all he and Dow could do to get him away from her and on his feet so they could move out, once they spotted the deputy slipping off with Case — which was the reason they were so damned far behind them. If they could've gotten Abe onto his horse a bit sooner, it might be all over by now, and they and Case would be long gone for Dodge or some other town.

But no, that woman-crazy Ladner had put them in the creek. One goddam thing for sure — when Case wanted to know why they were so long getting that deputy off his neck, it was going to be Abe Ladner doing the explaining.

"You still see them up ahead?" Dow asked.

"Did a piece back," Rockmond replied, listening to the coyote chorus that was drifting through the hills. He'd never liked the sound; it was too weird, too lonely, and it always started something crawling up his backbone. "Trees are sort've hiding them, but they're still there."

"Well, they got to pull up pretty soon. Horses are near beat."

"Reckon they will," Rockmond said. "Case's looking for us, so he'll be doing what he can to slow the deputy down and make it easy."

"Ain't much he can do."

"I know Case Medford. He'll come up with something. You reckon he knows we're here?"

"Likely. It's plenty quiet on a night like this. He could've heard us following."

"That deputy'll know it too, then, and be keeping a sharp eye out. You know who he is?"

"Nope. Ain't never seen him before. Could

be that Clayton City sheriff sent him down after Case."

Rockmond again changed positions, now resting his weight on the opposite leg. The need to continually be making an adjustment bothered him somewhat. It was as if he were getting too old to ride, and hell, he was only forty-two. But something was sure working on him. Time was when he could set a horse twenty hours or more straight running — and here now with no more than half that behind him he was hurting like all get out.

"No, don't think so," he said. "That marshal, Bishop, was aiming to do the delivering to John Saffire when he got plugged, so they had to pick somebody else. Had to be some jasper living right there in town. Saffire ain't had time to send down one of his deputies."

"Unless he was already there in the first place," Dow said. "Could be him and Bishop both figured to ride herd on Case."

Rockmond gave that thought, then nodded. "Probably the way of it. . . . There they are — topping out that little hill where them pines are."

Dow raised himself in his stirrups for a better view. He, too, was feeling the hardness of the saddle and, like Rockmond, wished mightily the deputy would call it quits for the night.

"Yeh, I got them spotted. Hell, we ain't no closer right now than we was a hour ago!"

"Can't make no time moving slow and quiet like we're having to do."

"Can't see no need for that either, Red. That deputy can't go nowheres, 'cepting straight on. He'd be a damn fool to head out across the hills — it'd slow him down too much. Why don't we put the spurs to these nags and try catching up?"

"You was just saying why — these horses ain't got a half mile run up this hill left in them."

Dow lapsed into silence, twisted about, glared angrily at Abe Ladner. Seeing the man asleep seemed to infuriate him, and reaching out, he tore a bit of branch from a close-by pine and flung it at his fellow rider. Ladner came up with a start as the sharp points of the needles clawed at his face.

"Hey! What the hell —"

"Set up and keep your eyes open!" Dow snarled. "We're fixing to move in on that deputy and Case, and you sure as hell better be ready."

Abe squared himself and strained to see ahead on the trail. "Where are they? I don't see nobody."

"They're there, all right," Dow replied sourly, "but I reckon it's mighty hard for you to see anything, less'n maybe it's a woman."

"Lay off me, Dow."

"I'd give a man odds that if a gila monster come crawling up your leg when you was fussing around with a gal, you'd never even know —"

"Goddam you, Dow, quit rawhiding me!" Ladner broke in angrily. "Just 'cause you can't have no luck with a woman don't give you leave to —"

"Shut up back there," Rockmond warned in a low voice. "Ain't no sense telegramming that deputy that we're on his tail — and we could be getting close. I think they've stopped."

"We keep a'following this here draw, I figure we'll come out on the trail right about where that old tree's leaning against that big rock," Eustace Cobb said.

"Sure be glad," Billy replied in a thankful voice.

Both boys were on foot and Eustace was leading the horse, more suited to the plow than the saddle, on which they had been riding double. The steepness and the loose surface of the slope had been such that the horse could barely manage on his own, let alone carry them on his broad back.

"What're we going to do when we catch up?" Billy continued.

"Plain can't do nothing 'til they stop. Now, I reckon they'll be making camp and rolling into their blankets when they get to the top of the hill. We'll do our doings then."

"You aiming to shoot that deputy? Ma said you —"

"I'm plenty dang tired of Ma telling me what to do and what I ain't to do!" Eustace flared. "I'm full growed and one of these here days I'm going to —"

The words hung in the quiet, cool air. Billy waited out a long breath. Then, "You'll do what?"

"I ain't sure, but I'll do something."

Billy wagged his head. "Just you try it and Ma'll cut the hide off'n you with that whip of her'n. She won't take no sass. What's the matter?"

Eustace had halted on a flat ledge that thrust itself horizontally from the wall of the wash. "Was watching the trail up there. Thought I counted three riders."

"Three?"

Eustace shrugged. "Must've been a shadow, or something. Was only two of them rode out — old Case and that there new deputy — and there sure ain't been nobody to join up with them," he said, and moved on.

Minutes later they reached the trail and were turning into it. Billy, sucking hard for wind, hunkered on his heels with a deep sigh.

"I'm glad that's done with."

Eustace nodded. "So'm I, but it saved us plenty of time, short-cutting like we done. I figure they ain't far ahead now, maybe even've pulled off and getting ready to bed down."

"You was thinking that back there on the hogback —"

The older Cobb swore fluently. "You expecting me to be perfect? You expecting me to know exactly what they'll be doing? All any man can do is guess and figure maybe."

"Didn't mean nothing again you, Eustace," Billy said, chastened. "I sure wish Ma'd thought of something else besides this of raising money. I don't like this shooting a deputy."

"Me neither," Eustace said, "and just maybe I won't have to. Maybe we can just sort've sneak in while he's sleeping, whop him across the head —"

"What'll we tell Ma?"

"Nothing, 'less she asks, then I can say I didn't want to waste no bullet so I just knocked his head in good. . . . Come on, let's keep going," he added, and swung up onto the saddle.

Billy sighed again, crawled up behind his

brother on the old horse. "You ain't going to get by lying to Ma. She can always tell."

"Dammit, there you go again, Billy! I ain't giving a hoot whether she believes me or not. If she's so all-fired full of wanting to have this here job done just so-so, then whyn't she come along with us?"

"Reckon 'cause she's a woman."

"Woman — ha! I figure she's more of a man than most, and if she was feared we'd not do —"

Abruptly Eustace brought the horse to a stop. He raised a hand for silence. The trail, a narrow silver path cutting across a wide flat at that point, veered sharply to the left as it avoided a dark shoulder of rock.

"What's the matter?" Billy asked in a low, breathless voice.

In reply Eustace slipped from the saddle, making no use of the stirrups. Waiting until Billy had also come off the aged gelding, he motioned again for silence, and moving to a nearby juniper, picketed the horse securely.

"Best we go on foot," he whispered. "Real quiet now. I got a feeling they've pulled up along them bluffs off'n the trail. Be a good camping place."

Billy made no answer. Close on his brother's heels, he followed him along the edge of the path until Eustace halted once more, this time on the crest of a low hill that sloped off on its yonder side onto a ledge that overlooked the ground beyond.

"Ain't no fire burning —" Billy began, and hushed immediately as Eustace pressed a hand against his mouth.

"There's somebody coming up from the bluffs. Two riders."

"What're they doing coming from —"

"Must've figured to camp, then changed their minds," Eustace interrupted again, straining to get a clear look at the approaching horsemen riding slowly along the base of the ledge. "It's them," he added, voice suddenly taut.

Billy drew back a step. He was filled with uncertainty now that the critical moment was at hand. "I'm scared," he murmured.

"I'm kind of scared, too," Eustace admitted, "but like Ma always says, them fellows ain't no different from us. Pull their pants on a leg at a time just like we do."

Squatting, he gave the oncoming riders a quick look and then edged near to the rim of the shelf.

"The deputy's in front," he said in a low voice. "Soon's he comes even I'll jump out on him, whop him good and solid on the head with Pa's pistol. You grab Medford's horse."

"How am I going to do that?" Billy asked, fearfully.

"You jump, too, right down there next to him and snatch the lines. Medford's hands are all chained together so he can't do nothing but try to ride off fast. You got to keep him from doing that while I take care of the deputy. Understand?"

Billy swallowed noisily. "Yeh, reckon so."

"Then get yourself ready. They're 'most here."

"How'll I know when to jump?"

"I'll holler *frog*. You hear me say that, you'll know it's time."

"All right, Eustace, but I ain't sure I can . . ."

"You'll be all right," the older Cobb whispered reassuringly, centering his attention on the two riders now only a wagon's length away. "Get ready —"

16

With Case Medford just ahead of him, Starbuck swung off the trail into the wash that cut west toward the bluffs. It wouldn't be necessary to go as far as the shadowy, irregular formation; he wanted only to remove his prisoner and himself a sufficient distance from the path to allow the three outlaws to pass without noticing. He felt no inclination, however, to make any explanation to Medford.

Moving along an overhanging ledge, he permitted Case Medford to continue until they were a long hundred yards from the trail, and then, in a small clearing fringed by thick brush and squat cedar trees, he called a halt.

"About time," the outlaw grumbled. "My tail's about growed to the saddle."

Shawn had come off his horse and was wrapping the lines about one of the trees. Stepping up to Medford, he helped him off and picketed the outlaw's bay alongside the sorrel. Drawing his rifle from its boot, he came about.

Medford was eyeing him sullenly in the bright moonlight. "What about my blanket? Ain't we sleeping here tonight?"

Starbuck returned the man's stare evenly. "All you have to do is sit down and keep your mouth shut."

The outlaw straightened slowly, began to nod. "I savvy what you're up to. You're aiming to let my boys ride on by and then get in back of them. I had me a hunch they was back there somewheres."

"Could be," Starbuck said noncommittally.

"Ain't going to work, Deputy," the outlaw said, wagging his head. "All I got to do is sing out —"

"Wouldn't even think about it," Shawn said quietly. "You even look like you're about to and I'll lay the butt of this rifle across your mouth so hard you'll have teeth in the back of your head."

Medford's confidence sagged. "Hell, you ain't about to do nothing like that. I'm your prisoner and it's your bounden duty to look out for me."

"My duty is to get you to Clayton City. Nobody told me you had to be alive," Shawn snapped, and pointed to a stump on the far side of the clearing. "Sit down over there and stay put."

Hard, glittering eyes on Starbuck, Case Medford shambled over to the rotting bit of tree and settled upon it. Apparently he was not entirely convinced that Shawn meant what he had said, but on the other hand he was equally uncertain as to the wisdom of making any brash moves to warn his friends.

Starbuck waited until the outlaw was seated, and then moved off a few steps, rifle cradled in his arms. The night was quiet, only the distant questioning of an owl and the continual yipping of the coyotes breaking the hush.

He could not see the trail from where they had stopped, the dense brush and thick-branched junipers and cedars growing along the gulch forming an effective screen. But he would hear the outlaws as they rode past, and he now turned his attention to that end.

He could not afford to miscalculate. He must permit the riders to move by and put a safe distance between him and his prisoner before striking out for the summit of the mountains looming in the east. Starting too soon would be a fatal mistake; one of the outlaws might glance back, see him and Medford crossing the trail or starting up the grassy slope, and sound an alarm.

Delaying too long could have similar disastrous results; the men could suddenly become aware that their friend Medford was no longer ahead of them, suspect a trick, and double back up the trail.

And Case Medford. He didn't feel at ease where the outlaw chief was concerned. The man could ignore his warning, gamble, yell out when his friends drew near. Case had everything to gain by attracting their attention — and a lump on the head or a mouthful of broken teeth would be preferable to the rope that was awaiting him in Clayton City.

Wheeling, Starbuck retraced his steps to the sorrel and, digging into his saddlebags, came up with an old square of cloth that he used as a towel. Ripping off a strip, he turned to Medford.

"On your feet."

The outlaw pulled himself upright slowly, suspiciously. Taking a key from his shirt pocket, Shawn released one of the iron cuffs, pulled the man's hands around behind his back, and replaced the manacle.

Medford grumbled a curse. "What the hell're you doing this for? I ain't —"

His angry question was choked off as Starbuck reached up, placed the strip of cloth over his mouth, drew it tight, and tied it securely.

"Not taking any chances on you crossing me up," Starbuck said, and he pushed the outlaw back down onto the stump.

Medford, eyes raging, muttered under the gag, but Shawn turned away and, taking up his rifle again, dropped back to the edge of the clearing. While he would have no qualms if it became necessary to silence the outlaw with a blow, he believed it was much wiser to eliminate the possibility entirely. Should Medford succeed in attracting his friends, it would come down to a shootout, and Starbuck would as soon avoid that.

He came to attention. Over to the south, below the wash with its overhanging shelf into which they had turned, he caught the sound of a voice. It was undoubtedly on the trail, could only mean the outlaws were approaching. At once he moved deeper into the fringe of brush, hoping to find a point where he would be afforded at least a glimpse of the riders as they passed.

A gnarled, twisted juniper offered possibilities. He glanced back to Medford. The outlaw had not stirred; he was sitting, hunched, on the stump. Propping his rifle against a clump of oak, Shawn climbed into the juniper. At most it raised him no more than half his height above the ground, but that was all that was necessary; a brief stretch of the trail, shining in the light of the moon as if wet, was now in view.

Almost immediately the outlaws broke into sight — three of them, riding single file, with the one bringing up the rear lagging behind somewhat. Slumped on his saddle, he was apparently dozing. His two companions were talking back and forth in guarded tones, evidently believing they were not too far behind Medford and waiting until they reached some specific point before closing in.

The faint *clop-clop* of the three horses echoed hollowly in the stillness as the outlaws drew abreast on the trail. Shawn cast a look over his shoulder at Case Medford. The outlaw had heard, was now on his feet. At once Starbuck dropped out of the juniper and, snatching up his rifle, returned to the clearing. Medford was shaking his head violently and mumbling under the gag covering his lips. Shawn, crossing to him, pushed him back onto the stump.

"Your friends," he said. "Three of them. Soon as they're down the trail we'll move out."

Case struggled to speak, his eyes hard and sparking. Starbuck, ignoring the outlaw's efforts, stood back, listened into the night at the departing horses, the sound of their hoofs gradually dying until there was only silence. Even then he continued to remain motionless, a tall, rigid shape in the streaming silver light until a full five minutes had elapsed, and then he came back to Medford.

"Get up," he ordered.

Sullen, the outlaw rose. Removing the gag from the man's lips, Starbuck released his locked hands from their behind-the-back position and restored them to their former place in front.

"This ain't going to do you no good," Medford said when he was finally able to speak. "Red and the others'll still be waiting for you."

"Red? Red who? Was three of them," Shawn said, fishing for information.

"Red Rockmond. Others'll be Abe Ladner and Dow Breedon. Mighty good friends of mine. You best remember their names, Deputy, 'cause you're sure going to be meeting up with them again!"

"Maybe," Shawn said indifferently. "That all the gang you've got left?"

"All I ever had, 'cepting for a couple more." Medford paused abruptly, cocked his head to one side. "I see what you're digging for! You're wondering if there'll be more besides them laying out there waiting for you. Well, you just keep on wondering, Deputy! Could be a half a dozen more of my boys figuring to take a hand and lay you by the heels."

Shawn laughed. "Hell, Medford, you never had that many friends in your whole life! Your kind never does."

"That's what you think, Deputy!"

"Makes no difference to me anyway. We won't be riding the trail. Get on your horse."

Medford started across the clearing, a frown on his whiskered face. "We aint? How you figure to —"

Starbuck pointed to the crest of the mountains in the east. "We're climbing over that, dropping down to the road on the other side."

Medford came to a halt, swore. After a moment he shook his head. "That won't fool them none either, not for long anyways. They'll come to that we ain't ahead of them, double back —"

"Probably all the way to Tannekaw," Shawn finished, motioning impatiently for the outlaw to mount. "I figured that, and by then we'll be getting close to Clayton City."

He waited until Medford was settled on the bay, and then, freeing the lines, he swung up onto his own saddle. Cutting his horse about, he rode in ahead of the outlaw, caught up the short rope he'd attached to the man's horse, and continued up the gully, following the same path along its floor they had earlier used.

He'd hang onto Medford's lead rope until they had crossed the trail and were well into the first stand of brush just in the event the outlaw, now desperate, decided to make a break and attempt to overtake his three friends.

They moved on through the hushed, silver-shot night. The owl had ceased his calling, stilled perhaps by the ceaseless barking of the coyotes, joined now by the lonely, more distinctive howl of a solitary wolf high up on the slope of the mountain toward which they were riding.

It would be no easy climb, Shawn realized, scanning first the shrub- and tree-studded lower area and then the higher, grass-covered grades. But they should have no real trouble, and if he was careful, they would have ample time to reach the crest.

A sudden dry scraping and the rattle of gravel on the ledge above him brought Starbuck to a halt. In the next fragment of time a high-pitched, almost hysterical voice shouted *frog*, and a dark shape came hurtling down from the overhang at him. And then Shawn felt his senses winging away as something hard and solid crashed into his head.

17

Tildy Cobb, sitting on the bench placed in front of the house, rocked gently back and forth in the cool, early morning. That was one thing she sure'n hell aimed to buy herself once she got her hands on all that money the law would be paying for Case Medford — a genuine, honest-to-God rocking chair.

She'd always wanted one, and Vic once had even tried to make one for her, using barrel staves for the rockers; but like everything else around the place, it had fallen apart. Now a store-bought one — that'd last for years.

Them danged boys ought to be coming unless they'd managed somehow to mess things up — which sure wouldn't be surprising. One thing that'd keep them watching their p's and q's — if they did mess up, they knew they was in for a hiding, and that ought to keep them thinking. It was about time the pair of them growed some responsibility. Hell-a-mighty! They couldn't figure on her being around forever, telling them what they ought and ought not to do.

Tildy came up off the bench, startling several of the chickens that had gotten through the hole in the wire enclosing their pen — a hole that Eustace had been told to fix a month ago.

The boys were finally coming — and they had Case Medford! By hell, they done something right, for a change! There they were, the two of them setting up there on Case's horse, proud as a banty rooster that had just mounted a big Orpington hen, as Vic would say, while Case, riding on old Jack, was trailing along behind.

"We got him, Ma!"

It was Billy. He was waving both arms and pointing at Medford. Eustace was saying nothing, just set there on that horse of Case's, ramrod-straight like he was General Ulysses S. Grant riding at the head of the Independence Day parade.

She'd keep that horse for the boy, give it to him for a present. He'd earned himself a reward, and the bay with its big saddle and fancy bridle would suit him just fine. He didn't have no use for money — would hardly know what to do with it if she give him some — and the sheriff she figured to find and turn Case over to wouldn't put up no fuss. Hell, where Case Medford was going he sure wouldn't be needing a horse.

Moving away from the bench, scattering the exploring chickens scratching about in the dust, Tildy walked deeper into the yard.

"What's this here all about, Tildy?" Medford shouted angrily as he pulled old Jack to a stop in front of her.

Eustace and Billy came off the bay and crowded up. "He's been hollering at us ever since we got him," the older boy said. "Kept saying he was a friend of you and Pa and that we ought turn him loose."

Tildy nodded pleasantly. "Howdy, Case," she said and spat a stream of tobacco juice at the chickens. "You're looking mighty pert for a jailbird."

Medford, gripping the loose horn of the ancient saddle girthed to old Jack, threw a leg over and dropped to the ground. Stepping up close to the woman he extended a manacled hand.

"Tell these here damn young'uns of yours to go fetch a hammer and a chisel and start cutting these irons off," he directed.

Tildy Cobb's thin gray lips, stained brown at the corners, parted to shape a half smile.

"Now, I sure can't do that, Case."

"Why not?"

" 'Cause I'm taking you to the law and getting me five thousand dollars."

Medford's dark features colored ever more,

and for a moment it looked as if he was on the verge of exploding. Then: "What these here two jackasses was telling me is straight! You aim to turn me in!"

"Sure do!"

Medford shook his head sadly. "Tildy, that ain't right, and you know it. We been friends for a lot of years, not counting the time your old man rode with me."

"Yeh, reckon he did, but that ain't putting no hay in the barn now. Business is business, Case, like I told my boys."

Medford swore in frustration, tried another tack. "Doing it'll be the biggest mistake you ever made, Tildy! I got three hard-case friends waiting for me up on the trail, and soon as I don't show up they're going to come looking for me. I'd sure hate to be in your shoes if that happens."

Tildy spat, transferred her attention to Eustace. "What about that, boy?"

"We didn't see no friends," he replied, and then frowning, scratched at the fuzz on his chin. "Just maybe we did. I figured it was Medford here, and the deputy when I first spotted them — but I counted three horses instead of two. Told Billy that."

"Then he figured he was a'looking at a shadow," Billy added. "It was a pretty far piece off, and we couldn't see so good."

"I reckon it was them friends he's talking about."

"They'd be," Tildy said. "What happened to them?"

"Just kept on going, far as I know."

"But they was following the deputy and Case," Billy said, struggling to organize his comprehension. "How'd they get in front of them?"

"Deputy probably pulled off the trail and set back for a bit, let them go on by," Tildy said.

"Just what he done," Eustace agreed. "We jumped him when he was coming out of a little draw. Him and Case'd been hiding out in it."

"What about the deputy? You fix him so's he won't be no bother?"

"Hell, no, they didn't!" Medford cut in before either Billy or Eustace could answer. "They let him get —"

"My boys're a telling this, Case," Tildy said coldly. "I'll thank you to keep your mouth shut. Go on, Eustace."

"We didn't have no chance, Ma," the older boy explained. "Me and Billy was waiting for him. Told Billy I'd take care of the deputy and he was to grab onto Case's horse so's he couldn't run away . . ."

"You kill that deputy or not?"

"No'm. Like I done said — there weren't no chance. I jumped down on him and hit him right smart across the head with Pa's pistol. It scared his horse and he went runnmg off into the brush with him a rocking and swaying on the saddle . . ."

"You see him fall?"

"No'm, sure never did. Dang horse got clean out of sight before I could do anything. Could be running yet."

"Ain't likely," Tildy said heavily.

It was a serious slip-up. The deputy could cause them a whole sackful of trouble, but maybe there was no need to worry about it right now. It would take him a spell to get his head straight if he'd been whopped as hard as Eustace claimed he had. Then he'd need to do some hunting around for tracks — and that'd sure take some time even if it was bright moonlight.

"Well, I reckon we don't have to worry about him much," she said after a bit. "He's going to have to find your trail, if he's the kind that can track, and by time he can get here, we'll be gone. Goes for Case's friends, too."

"Where we going — back to Tannekaw?" Medford asked quickly.

Tildy favored the outlaw with a withering look. "My ma didn't raise no damn fools,

Case, and I sure wasn't standing behind the door when the brains was passed out. I'm loading you up in the buckboard and hauling you across the line into Arizona."

"Arizona?"

"Yes, sir. Won't be nobody expecting you to be heading that way, and five thousand dollars of a Arizona sheriff's money is just as good as that sheriff's up in Clayton City."

Medford laughed, shrugged. "Hell, Tildy, if that there bounty money looks so all-fired big to you, I'll sweeten the pot and pay you a real big reward. Can easy make a deal —"

"Nope," Tildy Cobb cut in flatly. "I recollect Vic telling me once that you was slippery as hog guts in a bucket of slop when you got in a pinch. I'll just do my dealing with a lawman who —"

"I'd be raising the ante. Law says it'll pay you five thousand — I'll make it six. All you got to do is turn me loose."

"Nope," Tildy said. "I ain't about to let you euchre me out of what's rightfully coming to me."

"I ain't aiming to trick you. I'll stay right here and you can leave these irons on me. Just you send your boys after them friends of mine that'll be looking for me on the trail — expect you know them: Red Rockmond, and Dow Breedon and Abe Ladner. Bring them here, then I'll send Red after the cash. Means another thousand dollars for you, Tildy!"

Tildy Cobb glanced at her two boys. Both were staring at her — anxious, greedy, and dumber than a fence post.

"Wasting your wind, Case. You ain't got six thousand dollars, and you never had that much in your whole life, I expect. Was you to start scraping I misdoubt you could come up with sixty dollars — which sure is a hell of a ways from six thousand!"

"Well, now I ain't saying I got that much stashed away somewheres in a can, but there's a bank me and the boys figure to —"

"I'll do my dealing with a sheriff somewheres," Tildy said with a note of finality in her tone, and then she motioned to her sons. "Reckon you're hungry. Some vittles in there on the stove. Take Case in and let him eat, if he's of the notion, then bring him out to the shed."

Eustace frowned. "What for, Ma?"

Tildy moved up to the horses, gathered their lines into her clawlike hand, and started for the back of the yard.

"I'll have the buckboard hitched up," she said. "Want to get started for Arizona right soon."

18

Starbuck opened his eyes slowly. There was a stinging sensation along his neck and face and a thudding, dull pain in his head. He stirred, not fully conscious, and felt himself drop a short distance, but from a height sufficient to send a fresh wave of pain surging through him.

He lay quiet for a long minute, then finally twisted about and sat up, glancing about as reality returned to him. He had been lying across a clump of oak brush onto which he had either fallen or been thrown by his horse. The stiff, wiry shrub had probably saved him from serious injury, rewarding him only with a thorough scratching.

The sorrel . . . Shawn drew himself upright, extended his range of vision. If his horse was gone, he had trouble — and plenty of it. A sigh of relief slipped from his lips. The big gelding was standing off to one side, grazing contentedly on the thin grass.

Retrieving his hat, inwardly furious at himself for being caught off-guard, and making sure his pistol was still in its holster, he laid an unsteady course across the rough ground for the gelding. He reckoned he'd been out cold only a short while — a half hour, perhaps a bit more, so whoever it was that had jumped him and taken Case Medford could not be too far away.

Starbuck swore feelingly, the full realization of what had occurred — of the bare fact that he'd let someone take his prisoner from him — breaking through the slight haze that was fogging his brain.

He reached up and explored the side of his head tenderly as he sought to review what had taken place. Someone — or several men, he had no idea how many — had lain in wait on the ledge along which he had been passing with Medford on the return to the trail.

At a point not too far from the path a voice had suddenly yelled a word. It sounded like *frog*, but he wasn't exactly sure. In the next instant a figure had come slanting down off the ledge, almost knocking him off the saddle and striking him a solid blow on the head with something — probably the butt of a gun. As lights had exploded inside his brain he was briefly conscious of the frightened sorrel wheeling and rushing off into the trees. The next thing he knew he was sprawled across an oak clump that was pricking his skin.

Who the hell was it? Shawn rolled that question about in his mind as he climbed stiffly onto the sorrel. Certainly it could not have been any of Case Medford's three friends; they were well on down the trail by that time.

Some bounty hunter? Or was it Griff Mulky and Jig Docket who had been hanging around the jail? They seemed likely prospects. Mulky, for all his cooperative spirit, didn't ring true. He had been too set against Arlie Bishop, too envious. His abrupt change of heart was far from convincing.

Hell, it could have been anybody, Starbuck realized as he cut the sorrel about and doubled back for the wash where the attack had occurred. There'd been talk of bounty hunters, along with talk concerning Medford's gang, all just waiting for the chance to get their hands on the outlaw either to cash in on, or free.

Thus there was nothing to be gained by trying to figure out who it was that had taken Case Medford from him; the point was that it had occurred and it was up to him now to track them down and recover his prisoner. That it had not been a member of Medford's gang was good — the outlaw would still be a prisoner and that would make the job that lay before him a bit easier. Had it been

Rockmond and the other two Medford had mentioned, the outlaw would be free by now.

Starbuck reached the wash, halted, and studied the brightly lit area as he sought to get his bearings. The attack had taken place near the trail, he recalled, and he turned his attention to that area.

Moments later he reached the spot where he believed the dark shape had come sailing off the ledge onto him, and pulling the gelding to a stop, he dismounted. Directly beneath the highest part of the overhang was a confusion of hoof prints, undoubtedly made by the startled sorrel as he shied, wheeled, and finally broke and ran. There were marks also of Medford's bay, equally frightened, but for some cause unable to also flee.

Shawn dropped to his heels. The moon was bright, but puzzling out tracks was still difficult. There had been two men, as near as he could tell. It would appear one had jumped him, the other had come in, either from the ledge or up the draw to prevent Medford from escaping. Two men . . . Griff Mulky and Jig Docket?

Starbuck paused to give that consideration, and then resumed his study of the area. The pair had brought up a horse, a big-hoofed animal with badly worn shoes. There should be a third horse, it seemed, but he could find no prints indicating such. Likely it had been left up on the ledge or, when entering the gully, had walked along its edge, where leaves and weeds and the poor light combined to hide evidence of passage.

It was not difficult to trail the big horse, and Medford's bay, out of the wash and onto the trail. There Shawn, still on foot, again crouched and searched for an answer to the question now facing him: which direction had the bounty hunters taken?

Loose dust in the path provided the answer. Patiently working from the point where the big horse had emerged from the gully, Starbuck cast about until he located its hoof prints — heading back down the road. The discovery brought a frown to his face. That the bounty hunters would take a route which would lead them eventually to Tannekaw didn't make sense — unless, of course, they planned to cut off a safe distance this side of the settlement and swing either west for Arizona or east to Kansas. Such could be what they had in mind, he decided, but he'd better stay with the broad prints of the big horse until he knew definitely the choice they'd made.

It would cost him time but it could not be avoided. It was wiser to lose an hour in walking slow along the trail searching out the worn prints of the bounty hunter's horse — there evidently were two men riding double, since he was never able to pick up the tracks of the third animal — than take it for granted the party was headed back for the foot of the mountain and there find he'd made a mistake.

His decision had been the right one. Not more than a quarter mile later he became aware the tracks were no longer before him. At once Shawn wheeled and doubled back. Locating the prints once again, he pursued them carefully, shortly found where they had cut off the trail into a break in the brushy shoulder and struck down slope along a fairly large gully.

Starbuck climbed onto the sorrel and studied the area below him. It wouldn't be as difficult or as slow going now; the bounty hunters, with their prisoner, would be forced to keep to the canyonlike gash, thickly bordered with rocks and brush, that lay at the foot of the wash, once they reached it. Spurring the sorrel, he rode off the trail and began the descent.

The path, although steep, was not difficult, probably being one used by deer and other animals. The sorrel, however, was reluctant to hurry, the shadows and the loose footing turning him cautious. Once a bird, roosting in the low branches of a cedar that extended into the narrow path, and frightened by the big gelding's approach, exploded suddenly into the night directly in front of him. The sorrel jerked back, went down on his hindquarters. A moment later, still trembling, he recovered himself and continued.

They reached the bottom of the slope, and broke out onto the floor of the wide arroyo Shawn had noted from above. Halting, he dropped to the soft ground to reassure himself that he had not lost the trail. It was there — the deep, rounded shoe prints of the big horse and the smaller, more sharply defined set that would have been made by Case Medford's bay.

He looked ahead. In the deep, almost white sand the indentations were plainly evident as far as his eyes could reach in the pale light. He'd have no problems following the bounty hunters and their prize now — not so long as they stayed in the arroyo. Going back to the saddle, Starbuck pushed on, urging the gelding to a fast walk, the best the horse could do in the slack footing.

An hour later the bounty hunters and Medford veered away from the arroyo and swung into one that was considerably smaller. The hoof prints were not as definite on the more solid surface, but Starbuck had only minimal difficulty in keeping them in sight —

although on several occasions he did halt, dismount, and examine the ground closely to be certain he was on the right course.

Near morning, as first light began to brighten the eastern sky, he found himself leaving the high country and entering an area of small, round-topped, grassy hills which, like green bubbles, melted gradually until they dissolved into a broad valley. There he pulled up short in a fringe of cedars that marked the change.

Before him was an aged, weatherworn shack in the advanced stages of dilapidation. Several sagging sheds lay beyond it, and in the littered yard behind stood a buckboard to which a dozing plow horse was hitched. Nearby was Case Medford's bay.

19

Immediately Starbuck cut back, and circling, came up to the old house from its blind, north side. Taut, he slipped from the saddle, and tieing the sorrel to a handy post, the solitary remainder of what had once been a rail fence, he moved quietly toward the rear of the structure.

Whoever the bounty hunters were that had taken Medford from him, he was certain now they were not Griff Mulky and Jig Docket. And it was unlikely they lived in the old shack. Men who made their living at tracking down and capturing wanted outlaws for the reward they'd receive would not spend their time here when they could be enjoying money and possibly getting a line on other wanted and valuable criminals in one of the larger towns.

What seemed most feasible was that something had happened to the horses of the bounty hunters and they had gone to the shack in search of help — but they had evidently been using the big horse that was now hitched to a buckboard. Starbuck, halted at the corner of the house, considered that puzzle. Had they, by accident, encountered someone along the trail who had been riding the —

Shawn's theorizing came to a stop. The sagging screen door, its wire torn loose and bulging in several places, had swung open. Medford, chain cuffs still linking his wrists, stumbled as if pushed into the open. Behind him came two nearly grown boys in ragged, patched clothing — the larger, older of the pair holding a pistol in his hand. Bringing up the rear was a woman.

Stringy hair hanging about her shoulders, threadbare dress hanging limply from her emaciated frame like a wet rag, a man's heavy shoes on her feet and a battered hat on her head, she stepped into the clear, turned a dour, lined face to one side, and splattered the bole of a nearby tree with a quantity of tobacco juice.

"You keep that horse right close behind us now, Eustace," she said in a crackly voice. "I'll be busy driving so you watch out for somebody following."

The larger of the boys nodded, pleased with his assignment. "Yes, Ma," he said and moved toward Case Medford's bay.

"Now, Billy, I want you hunching right behind Case, here," the old woman continued, now talking to the smaller and apparently younger boy. "I put a stick of wood there in the buckboard. He makes a move to do anything but set quiet-like on the seat beside me, you whop him a good one on the head. Hear?"

"Yes'm," Billy replied.

The woman turned to Medford, halted a few steps ahead of her. Evidently they were acquainted, as she had called him by his given name.

"All right, climb aboard!"

Arms folded, Starbuck moved from the corner of the shack, along its wall. He was compelled to gamble on there being no one else inside the structure, and he was minimizing the danger by keeping close to it.

"Never mind, Medford," he called.

The old woman and her two boys whirled in alarm. The outlaw came slowly about, laughed.

"Told you, Tildy. Said you'd never get away with grabbing me. You should've listened to that deal I was trying to make you."

"Shut up, Case!" the old woman snapped, her face stiff with anger. She glanced at the boys — at the older one standing crouched, pistol in hand — and brought her hard-surfaced eyes back to fix on Starbuck. Delivering herself of her cud, she said, "Who the hell're you, mister?"

"The man your boys took Medford from."

"He's the deputy," the outlaw added. "The one that dumb brat there never put no bullet into. Deputy, this here lady is Tildy Cobb, an old friend of mine. She's aiming to collect the bounty for herself."

Medford's voice was dry, weighted with sarcasm and forced humor.

"You're goddam right I am, Deputy," Tildy stated, bobbing her head, "and if you don't want your hide shot plumb full of holes you'll get the hell out of here right now and mind your own business."

"Happens Medford is my business," Shawn said, coolly.

"He ain't no more! We took him from you fair and square. Belongs to me — me and my boys."

Case Medford laughed again. "She's looney as a broomtail grazing on locoweed!"

Starbuck lowered his arms. There was no way of knowing, but the boy glaring at him so hatefully could be good with a gun — and he already had it in his hand. Best he take no chances, be ready.

"I'm taking back my prisoner," he said in a quiet, level voice. "Want you to stand where you are and give me no trouble. . . . Medford, come over here to me."

"No!" the old woman shrilled. "Eustace, if he takes one step, you shoot that deputy right in the belly!"

The outlaw hesitated, looking at Starbuck questioningly. Over in a nearby pen several hogs were rooting about in a slime that was filling the still air with a heavy, sickening odor. Shawn nodded to Tildy.

"Lady, you'd best back out of this now before somebody gets hurt."

"I ain't about to!" Tildy shouted. "Case belongs to me, same as that five thousand dollars I'm collecting when I turn him over to a sheriff — and you or nobody else's going to cheat me out of it!"

It was pointless to argue with the old woman. Starbuck swung back to Medford. "Come on over here."

The outlaw ducked his head at Eustace. "That kid's crazy enough to shoot —"

"That's my worry."

Medford gave that thought, apparently concluded he had nothing to lose either way it went, and started across the yard. Tildy Cobb whirled to Eustace.

"Shoot, goddammit! Shoot the deputy!"

The boy's arm came up. Before he could trigger his weapon Starbuck drew and fired. Eustace staggered back and fell, his free hand clutching at his shoulder. There was a long breath filled only with the echoes of Shawn's forty-five, and then Tildy broke and ran to the side of her boy. Crouching over him, she gathered him into her arms.

"You — you killed him!" she screamed at Starbuck. "You goddam badge-toting bastard, you killed him!"

Shawn, with Medford now close by, waited for the tirade to end. When it was over he shook his head.

"He's not hurt bad — but you better hear this. Any of you gets in my way again and I won't be so careful where my bullet goes. Billy," he added, waggling his weapon at the younger boy, "get over there and help your ma. I want you all inside that shed back of the pigpen."

Billy, frozen during the altercation, hurried to his mother, and together they got Eustace onto his feet and started for the old shed. Midway Tildy stopped and made as if to retrieve the pistol dropped by her older son.

"Leave it," Starbuck ordered.

The woman turned her weathered, hopeless face to him. All the belligerence was gone from her now, and she asked only mercy.

"Ain't got but that one gun, Deputy. Belonged to my man, and he's dead. Sure'd be obliged if you'd let me keep it."

"You let her pick that iron up and she'll kill

you dead with it!" Medford warned. "That old crow's worse'n a riled rattlesnake!"

"You'll get it back — later," Shawn said, and again motioned the Cobbs toward the sagging old shelter.

Tildy's thin shoulders stirred. "This here boy's bad hurt. Sure take it as a favor if you'd fix him up —"

Starbuck ignored the woman's plaintive words and, crossing the yard, picked up the pistol and thrust it under his belt. Holstering his own weapon, he waited until a resigned Tildy, with her two boys, were in the shed; then, gathering in the reins of Medford's horse, he led it to where the outlaw was standing.

"Let's go," he said. "Left my sorrel over back of the house."

Medford moved off willingly, undoubtedly glad to be free of Tildy Cobb's hands. They came to the sorrel, and Shawn, allowing the outlaw to first get onto the saddle, stepped wearily up to his horse and mounted. It had been a long day and night. He was feeling the drain on his strength.

"Which way we going?" the outlaw asked in a voice that reflected his worn condition also.

"Same as we came in —"

"How about that there gun of mine?" Tildy called from the shed. "You told me . . ."

"Wait for an hour, then send Billy up the draw for it," Starbuck replied. "I'll leave it alongside the trail. . . . Pull out, Medford."

20

The horses were already tired when Starbuck, riding behind Case Medford, began the return journey to the trail. They moved slowly and with effort along the rising course, and he halted periodically to give them rest — and to ease his own aching bones and muscles.

"Whyn't we just pull off here and lay over a spell?" Medford suggested when they came to the large arroyo off which the smaller wash they followed turned.

Shawn drew Tildy Cobb's pistol from his belt and dropped it in the center of the junction where it could not be overlooked.

"We'll have to keep going until we're back on the trail," he said. "Don't much like this country."

"Why? What difference it make?"

"Too easy for somebody to move in on a man. Like to do my camping where I can pretty much see what's around me."

"You thinking them Cobbs'll make another try?"

Shawn grinned wryly. "That old woman's tough as a boot, and she sure wants that bounty money. I wouldn't put it past her. But it's not her so much — it's the others hanging around hoping to get their hands on you."

Medford's chin, sunk into his chest, came up quickly. "There somebody else trailing us?"

"Bound to be. . . . Keep moving."

The outlaw settled back and urged his weary horse into motion. Starbuck swung in behind him. They were in the wide arroyo now, with its loose sand floor that, coupled with its steady climbing grade, took double toll of the horses' strength and called for frequent stops. Finally, when they reached the point where the path cut away from it and began the final, much steeper ascent to the trail itself, Shawn halted.

Immediately Case Medford raised an objection. "This ain't no place to pull up," he declared, sourly. "Nothing but rocks and sand and weeds —"

"These horses will never make it to the top unless we give them rest — an hour, at least," Starbuck replied, swinging off the saddle.

Leading the sorrel to a level area in the arroyo, he tied the gelding to a clump of Apache plume and loosened the cinch. Turning then to the outlaw's bay, he led him in beside the sorrel, secured him, and released his tightly pulled saddle band also. That done, he poured a small amount of water from his canteen into the mouth of each and then returned to Medford. The outlaw had found himself a spot at the edge of the arroyo and, stretched out full length beside the low bank, was already asleep.

Starbuck, eyes leaden and heavy also, studied the man for a time. He was reluctant to leave the outlaw unattended, even though manacled, while he caught a few minutes' sleep himself. Case could be shamming, just waiting for him to drop off and afford him his opportunity to escape.

But Starbuck knew he had to rest; it was much riskier fighting it. He had planned to return to the main trail before setting up camp and, after taking proper precautions, giving in to the demands of his body; but the condition of the horses had put an end to that idea.

He'd simply have to postpone his nap and take his chances, he decided. They'd not be there long enough for him to rope the outlaw as securely as he intended to do when they halted for a lengthy camp — and he'd be foolish not to even for a brief time. He could hold out, and once they were back on the trail and reached a place where it would be safe to set up, he'd make up for the sleep he'd lost.

Meanwhile, he'd move about, do a bit of thinking and planning. There seemed little point now in crossing the mountains to the main road. It was logical to assume that Medford's friends — Rockmond, Breedon, and Abe Ladner — had, hours ago, realized their error and doubled back with the expectation of encountering Case and him somewhere along the way.

When that failed, it was equally logical for them to think that he had taken Medford over the mountains, as he had earlier planned to do, and that they were on the Clayton City road. The only course left open to them, if they intended to free Medford, would be to do likewise.

It was all speculation, of course, but it seemed reasonable to Shawn, and after he had mulled it about in his mind for a time, weighing the probabilities, he concluded it would be wiser to stay on the trail and hope the outlaws were on the opposite side of the towering hills.

An hour later, after having a look down the arroyo to assure himself the Cobbs were not venturing another attempt to claim Medford, he tightened the saddle cinches, roused the outlaw, and resumed the path that led upward to the trail. The rest had benefitted the horses greatly and they made it to the top with no difficulty, although by the time it was accomplished, weariness had again set them to trembling.

But Shawn felt he now had everything going his way. He had not liked being down below the trail in the canyon-like arroyo where the horses were compelled to move slowly and a man found himself at a disadvantage; the odds would have all been against him if Medford's friends or any bounty hunters had discovered them there and stationed themselves with rifles along the rim.

Shortly after they had gained the upper area and had passed the ledge of rock where Tildy Cobb's two boys had made their bid, he pointed to a small grove of pines and lesser growth a quarter mile off to their right.

"Aim to pull up there, rest out the day," he advised Medford. "Good grazing for the horses."

"Can use some grub myself," Medford said. "That old woman had a mess of something cooked up but it wasn't fit to eat."

"I'll fix a meal," Starbuck said, "and then I'm tieing you up and getting some sleep."

He had expected immediate objections from the outlaw but Case Medford only shrugged, apparently too worn out himself to find fault with the idea.

* * *

Late in the afternoon, rested and fed, they saddled up and rode on, paralleling but keeping off the trail where passage would be conspicuous except when the ragged contour of the country forced them, for the sake of the horses, to use the easier, established course.

Starbuck did not let up at sundown but continued well into the moonlit night, drawing to a halt, finally, when their mounts again began to show weariness. They made camp on the side of a lesser mountain, selecting a grassy coulee where a spring provided water for the horses and enabled Starbuck to replenish the diminishing supply in the canteens.

Case Medford, clearly disturbed and disappointed by the failure of his friends to put in an appearance, had little to say, and when that next morning they rode out, he seemed resigned to the fate that awaited him in Clayton City.

"Never figured the boys'd give up on me," he said later, as they pressed on at a steady pace. "Things sure ain't like they used to be. Was a time when they'd a gone to hell for me — same as I'd do for them."

"Men change," Shawn had commented absently, but he was not abandoning his vigilance — was instead, sharpening it.

The nearer they came to their destination the greater the danger, he believed — if not from Medford's bunch, from the bounty hunters who could be waiting his arrival with the outlaw somewhere along the last miles that led into the settlement.

That Clayton City was his goal had been common knowledge, and it was only reasonable to think that there would be some people electing not to make any attempt to take Medford from him in the mountains, where they could find themselves at a disadvantage, but to set their ambush at a short but safe distance from the town.

He'd need to be doubly watchful on that last day before reaching the settlement, and when the night preceding it came, he made preparations — checking his rifle to be certain the magazine was full and that the weapon was in good working order, cleaning his pistol, refilling the empty loops in his gunbelt with cartridges, and fashioning his rope into a tether with which he could effectively control Case Medford.

The outlaw protested loudly that next morning when Shawn placed the loop about his arms, clamped them about his waist with a good knot, and then anchored the trailing end of the rope to the sorrel's saddle.

"How the hell you figure I can ride all

trussed up like this?" he demanded. "You got these goddam chains on me — ain't that enough?"

"Not far as I'm concerned," Starbuck replied as he climbed onto the gelding. "Won't be for long, anyway. Ought to reach Clayton City around noon."

Shawn stayed well clear of the trail while taking advantage of every rise to pause and have a thorough look at the country. Once he saw two riders well back up in the hills, and this drew his close attention for several minutes. They appeared to be moving slowly, however, and at such a pace, they would fall far short of overtaking him and his prisoner before the settlement could be reached.

Near midmorning, as they were breaking out of the higher hills and angling for a not too distant valley above which smoke was hanging like a dirty, cotton cloud in the sky, Starbuck saw the faint trace of the main road cutting in from the east to lay a narrow band across the flats for Clayton City.

If he was to have trouble it would come soon, he thought — in the brushy, cedar- and juniper-studded broken land that stretched between the high country they were leaving and the settlement. Reaching back, he drew his rifle and laid it across his lap; then, taking hold on the rope that connected him with the outlaw, he gave it a sharp, reminding jerk.

"Anything starts," he called to Medford, a length ahead of him, "you keep riding straight down the trail for town."

Case Medford, slumped on his saddle, pulled himself erect and swept the surrounding area with a quick glance.

"You expecting somebody, Deputy?" he asked, his tone once again taunting and derisive.

Starbuck's features were taut. "Just mind what I tell you — and keep remembering, you're the first man under my gun."

The outlaw shrugged, leaned forward against the rope as if to gain slack. "Reckon I ain't about —"

The crackle of guns cut into Case Medford's words. Immediately Starbuck swung his rifle up and into line. Three riders had broken from a brushy wash a hundred yards or so ahead. They were coming at him and Medford from two sides.

"By God — it's old Red!" the outlaw shouted gleefully. "And there's Abe and Dow — your goose is sure cooked now, Deputy!"

Starbuck raked the big sorrel with his spurs, and as the horse began to lengthen his stride, he folded an arm, steadied the rifle upon it, and took aim at the nearest of the oncoming outlaws, all hunched low and firing pistols.

Their bullets were falling short, the range being too far to be effective.

Starbuck pressed off a shot. The man he'd targeted threw up his hands and spilled from the saddle. His two friends slowed, and as Shawn levered a fresh cartridge into the chamber of his weapon, both began to veer off. At once Case Medford began to yell curses at them, the words riding above the drumming hoofs of the horses, now running at top speed down the slight grade.

Crouched low, Shawn watched the outlaws swing off into the brush. It would be at close range now, he realized, and then, sliding the rifle back into its boot, he drew his pistol. Abruptly bullets began to whip past him, pluck at his jacket, dig into the dust around the sorrel's driving feet.

He caught a glimpse of one of the outlaws riding parallel and snapped a shot at him. He missed. A moment later the man broke out into an open space between tall clumps of rabbitbush. Shawn fired instantly. The outlaw sagged, clutched at his side, and swerved off.

Starbuck flinched as white hot heat seared across his leg. He jerked about, saw the last of Medford's friends bearing in on him from an angle. Flat on the saddle, the man was firing as he came. His strained features, dark, lean, hawklike, were definite through the thin pall of dust.

Shawn leveled his forty-five, held to compensate for the motion of the rushing sorrel. A second bullet streaked his forearm, whipped dust from his sleeve. He steadied himself and pressed off his shot.

The outlaw sank lower on his saddle. The pistol he was holding tipped, fell from his hand. His hat came off, and then he tumbled from his swerving horse to the ground.

Shawn took a deep breath and settled back — but it might not be over yet, he realized; the town was now close, but there was still time for others to make an attempt. Letting the sorrel race on in the wake of Medford and his bay, he reloaded his weapon, set his teeth against the burning in his leg, and probed the steadily flattening land about them for other riders. Ahead, Case Medford was cursing in a wild, frustrated way.

A hard grin broke Starbuck's tight lips. The first of Clayton City's houses loomed suddenly on his left as the trail made a sweeping curve around a low butte. He could see the street, see people looking toward him — wondering, no doubt, what the shooting had been about and why all the hurry.

His grin widened as he slipped the forty-five back into its holster. He'd made it.

21

"Was the way Bishop said he wanted it," John Saffire declared.

The lawman was sitting at his desk in the Clayton City sheriff's office with the five thousand dollars bounty money for Case Medford, safely behind bars, in a neat stack of bills before him.

Starbuck swore quietly. It was late afternoon. His leg had been doctored, he'd had a good meal, and he was preparing to head back for Tannekaw. Why the hell had Arlie insisted on collecting the reward in cash? Was he planning to ride on, and not return to Tannekaw? Planning to begin a new life somewhere else — perhaps with the other woman that Carla Bishop had mentioned? Shawn reckoned no one would ever know the answer to that.

"Any chance getting it changed back into a bank draft?" he wondered.

The lawman shook his head. "Sure ain't, leastwise not for a couple of days. Cable, man that runs the bank, is out of town — not that it'd make a hell of a lot of difference. Draft can be cashed easy enough."

Packing five thousand in cash wasn't at all to Shawn's liking, but it would seem he had no choice, and, as Saffire had pointed out, a draft was almost as negotiable.

"You aim to lay over?"

"No, I'll go on. There anybody around know I'll be carrying all this cash besides you?"

Saffire, a lean, graying man with steady black eyes, thought for a moment and shook his head. "Don't think so, but I won't swear it couldn't've leaked out. Word came from Bishop some time back and probably was forgot until you came riding in after all that shooting."

"Wasn't my idea," Starbuck said dryly.

The sheriff nodded. "Didn't mean it that way. You figure to ride out now?"

Shawn began to collect the packs of currency, some of it in old bills, some fairly new, and stuff it inside his shirt. Later he'd place it in his saddlebags, covering it with pieces of clothing, his cooking equipment, items of grub, and all else available. Damn Arlie Bishop anyway! What might have been an easy, worry-free trip back to Tannekaw was now going to be one during which he'd need to be on guard.

"Right away," he said, answering the lawman's question. "Got some personal business that needs taking care of soon as possible. . . . Obliged to you for the favors — getting me patched up and such."

"The thanks go to you," Saffire said. "We owe you plenty for bringing in Medford — and getting rid of that gang of his at the same time."

"Matter of luck," Starbuck said, and turning to the door, added, "So long."

John Saffire nodded. He smiled in his tight, brief way, and Starbuck stepped out onto the walk and crossed to where the sorrel was waiting. Glancing about, he noticed no one paying any undue attention to him; mounting, he swung off into the street and pointed south. He'd stick to the road, he had already decided; it would be faster, and alone without Medford to divide his attention, he could keep a sharp watch for trouble should there be anyone intending to relieve him of the bounty money. Despite Sheriff Saffire's assurance that it was unlikely anyone in Clayton City would entertain such an idea, the removal of all threat from Medford's gang, and the almost dead-certain impossibility of Tildy Cobb and her boys showing up again, Shawn felt he'd best take no chances; the money would cease to be a worry only when it was out of his hands and in possession of Carla Bishop.

He camped that night after riding deep into the eastern slopes of the mountains, beside a stream that came rushing down from the high peaks, gleaming distantly like soft gold in the moonlight.

Both he and the sorrel enjoyed a good rest, and Shawn was up, had finished his meal, and was on the road again shortly before first light had started to fill the empty sky. That day passed also without incident, the only travelers he encountered being a man with his wife and family in a canvas-covered wagon moving lock, stock, and barrel to Montana.

To his casual question concerning other pilgrims on the road, the man said they had noticed two riders the previous day. They were camped off to one side and he'd not been afforded a close look at them, but they appeared to be cowhands — probably moving about in search of work.

Starbuck received the comments with a certain amount of relief. He guessed Tildy Cobb had actually done him a favor in creating a delay. Outlaws and bounty hunters lurking along the route to Clayton City awaiting his appearance with Case Medford had evidently been thrown into confusion by his failure to arrive at the expected time.

They had been compelled to change their

plans, as had Medford's three friends, and had then missed out entirely. And if they had later stationed themselves on the flat near the settlement, Case Medford's gang had once again upset their hopes by making their last, desperate try.

He wondered about Griff Mulky and the man with the odd walk, Jig Docket. He'd been wrong about Mulky, he guessed. The deputy had been sincere, and his change of heart where Arlie Bishop was concerned, genuine. He'd suggest to Carla that she give the deputy a small part of the reward — a hundred dollars, perhaps; that would go far in making a good friend of Griff.

His second night's camp was on a ledge that overlooked the road, and while there was no close-by stream or spring to furnish water, it was comfortable. He lay awake near a low fire, wrapped in his blanket and listening to the yapping of coyotes while he thought about Ben.

As soon as he returned to Tannekaw and relieved himself of the money due Carla Bishop, he'd spend time going through Arlie's desk in the hope of coming across something that would reveal what it was the lawman had to tell him.

There could be a letter, a scribbled notation, a few words Arlie had jotted down that would answer his question. Ben — dead. Starbuck hadn't accepted that yet, and he wouldn't until he knew, firsthand, that it was true. . . . And if so —

Shawn considered the possibility. It meant that everything would change for him — his efforts to catch up with Ben, his way of life, his outlook for the future, his own personal plans. The thought left him with an emptiness, and he was finding it difficult to accept. . . . And he wouldn't; he'd not go into it — not yet. If it proved true, facing it would come soon enough.

He made good time the next day, and by riding well into the moonlit night, only slightly less bright than at the start, he put himself in position to reach Tannekaw before the following noon.

He supposed he'd been fortunate in encountering no more trouble than he had — the Cobbs and Medford's friends, Breedon, Ladner, and Redmond — and he hoped he'd not have to ever again undertake a task of similar responsibility, but there'd been no way out of it. Carla being who she was had made refusal out of the question; he'd felt he could do no less than help her under the circumstances.

Starbuck pulled the sorrel down to a walk, a sudden wariness coming over him. He was passing through a stretch of road that was hemmed in closely on both sides by thick brush and trees. He had seen motion. It could have been a deer or some other large animal, but nevertheless he fixed his attention on the area that had drawn his eyes.

A moment later his hand dropped to the pistol on his hip, came up fast as a rider broke into view. Starbuck paused. There was something familiar about the man, and then as he came into the center of the road Shawn saw that it was Griff Mulky.

Frowning, Starbuck lowered his arm, but he did not holster his weapon; he simply allowed it to hang against his leg.

"Been waiting for you!" Mulky called, pulling to a halt.

Shawn considered the deputy coolly. If the lawman had planned an escort, it seemed he would have put in an appearance farther up the road.

"Why?" Starbuck asked, blunt and to the point.

"Got a little business with you," Mulky said with a broad smile. "Now, just you let that gun you're holding drop. Jig's standing across the road from me and he's got a rifle aimed straight at your head."

He hadn't been wrong about the deputy after all, Starbuck realized, as tension drew his faculties to wire-taut pitch — only wrong about when Griff and Jig Docket would make their move. He had thought they would follow, attempt to bushwhack him along the trail and take Case Medford from him. Instead they had chosen the easier way — holding off until he had the money. Now they had only to take it from him and strike out for some distant part of the country.

But they didn't have it yet. Unmoving, Starbuck studied the deputy. Jig Docket perhaps was holding a bead on him but he still had his own gun in his hand. He needed only a fleeting instant to throw himself backward off the sorrel and then, shielded by the horse, put a bullet into Mulky — who, in his supreme confidence, had not troubled to draw his weapon. Then he could deal with Docket.

"You hear me?" Mulky demanded, raising his voice, "Drop that there gun, then toss that money you collected for Medford over here to me. It's cash, and I know 'cause I seen the letter Bishop wrote that sheriff —"

"Then what?" Shawn asked, stalling for the right moment.

"Want you to turn around, head off up that draw back of you —"

"So you can put a bullet in my back, that it?"

"What difference it make where you get it?

Dead's dead. . . . Keep watching him, Jig. Been told he's quicker'n greased lightning with that iron of his — and he ain't shed it yet."

"You and Docket have this all schemed up from the start?"

"Sure. Made up my mind that bounty money was going to be mine — leastwise most of it. Was aiming to take care of Bishop ourselves 'til somebody changed that by killing him. Then you come along. Figured to ask you to take Medford to Clayton City but you obliged me by coming up with the idea yourself. You dropping that gun or —"

Griff Mulky's words died in the sudden crack of a pistol shot. As he rocked back on the saddle and began to fall, the weapon spoke again — the report coming from a short distance down the road. Abruptly Jig Docket staggered into view. The rifle he held was dangling uselessly from one hand; the other was pressed to his chest. The rifle dropped to the ground, and Docket, struggling, managed to gain the center of the road and there collapsed.

Starbuck, motionless on the saddle, rode out a long breath, eyes searching the brush where the pistol shots had come from. Gun cocked but still at his side, the sharp odor of burnt powder drifting to him, the stirred dust from the hoofs of Griff Mulky's shying horse hanging in the warm air, he waited.

And then from a point some half a dozen strides nearer than expected, a man stepped into the open. Starbuck recoiled as surprise rolled through him. It was Dave Kerry.

22

A hard smile down-curved Kerry's lips. He looked neat and trim, and his boots shone dully beneath the thin film they had collected. The pistol he held was leveled. It was silver-plated, glinted in the sunlight; it probably had pearl handles, Shawn thought, and was what could be expected of the man. But it was no small caliber, hide-out gun; it was either a forty-four or a forty-five.

"We meet again," Kerry said in his cool, polite way. . . . "I'll take that money."

Starbuck made no move to comply. He shook his head. Off on the slope above him a jay was scolding noisily.

"Figured you for a friend of the Bishops — especially Carla."

Kerry shrugged. "Man makes the best of his opportunities. That's how he gets along in this world. She's a beautiful woman, and Bishop was a fool. Neglected her. Only natural that some man step in to take his place. Happened to be me."

It was all coming together in Starbuck's

mind now. "That why you killed Bishop — because he warned you to stay away from his wife?"

"Saw me leaving the house one day. He was supposed to be gone from town. It was a trick to trap me. He called me into his office about a week later, saying he wanted to talk. Went out of his head and started to draw on me. I beat him to it. Had no choice."

Kerry paused. His smile tightened into a hard line relieved only at the corners. "Expect that satisfies your curiosity. Now — the money —"

Shawn stirred on the saddle. He wasn't sure if Dave Kerry knew that he had his pistol out and was holding it at his side; as it now stood, each holding a weapon, they would start even when — and if — a shootout came. He doubted Kerry was aware of his readiness, however. The sorrel was standing broadside to the man.

"Seems folks were wrong about you having plenty of money," Shawn said, continuing to stall. He needed to somehow take the man off-guard; Kerry had his weapon up and leveled. "That what you were after all along?"

Kerry's shoulders again shifted. "Cash is something a man always is in need of. Getting that bounty money came along later — after

Bishop caught that outlaw, and put himself in line to collect."

"You figure to ambush him when he came back from Clayton City?"

"Was the way I had it planned, only his pushing me into killing him changed that. That five thousand in cash or a bank draft?"

Dave Kerry's wariness seemed to be diminishing slightly. "Carla told me it was you that suggested I deliver Medford to the sheriff in Clayton City —"

"You, or anybody else. Made no difference to me, but she set such store by you that I thought it would be smart to play along with her." Kerry hesitated, ducked his head at Griff Mulky's prostrate figure.

"I didn't want him in on it, though. Had him figured out from the start. He would have collected the bounty and kept on going — and he just might have been able to give me the slip."

Kerry moved a few steps farther into the road. "Been enough talk, Starbuck. Hand over the money — or the draft, whichever it is. I don't intend to spend any more time explaining things that won't matter to you five minutes from now. Only sorry it has to be you that dies. Under other circumstances we probably could've become friends."

"Doubt it," Shawn said quietly.

Kerry's jaw tightened and his eyes flickered briefly. "Have it your way. Where've you got the money?"

"Saddlebags."

"All right, climb down slow and easy, untie them, and toss them to me."

Starbuck nodded. "You giving me a chance to draw?"

"We'll see about that later. First I want the money, then you're going to drag the deputy and his gimpy friend off into that gully behind you and bury them so's they won't be found — at least for a time. I don't want anybody connecting their disappearance with mine. Then we'll talk about you. . . . Easy, now."

"You're calling the shots," Shawn murmured.

If he was to come out of this one alive, he would have to make his move now, Starbuck realized. Grasping the saddlehorn with his right hand, and careful to keep the left out of Kerry's sight, Shawn threw his leg over the sorrel, and with great deliberation, dismounted.

The instant his heels struck solid ground all casualness vanished. With the gelding between him and Dave Kerry, he pivoted, dropped to a crouch. His gun came up fast.

"Hold it!" Kerry shouted in sudden alarm and fired a hurried shot.

Starbuck was pivoting away, going down full length into the loose dust of the road, triggering his weapon as he did. His first bullet caught Dave Kerry in the chest. The man took a stumbling step backward, a puzzled frown pulling at his face as if he could not understand how he could have allowed himself to be outwitted when he was holding all of the high cards. He came to an uncertain stop, hung for a long moment, and then his knees buckled and he fell.

Jig Docket was not dead. Starbuck had discovered that when he prepared to load the three men onto their horses and continue to Tannekaw. It was a mortal wound, but the man did live long enough after reaching the settlement to tell what had happened — not only confessing his and Griff Mulky's part but relating what he had heard Dave Kerry say as well.

Starbuck made his explanation as well, filling in what Docket had omitted, and then, still in the saddle, rode on to the Bishops' house. He was anxious to rid himself of the money and end the affair.

"I'm sorry about Kerry," he said after telling Carla of the man's duplicity. "Hard to say right out like this, but I guess he just used you."

The woman's smile was bitter. "I wasn't fooled by him. I knew right along, I suppose, but I was lonely and he gave me comfort — something I needed badly. He didn't mean anything to me, but I think I found something in Arlie's desk that may mean something to you."

Starbuck looked at her closely. "About my brother?"

Carla nodded, turned to the mantle above the fireplace, and took down a folded sheet of paper. She handed it to him. It was an ordinary poster of the sort circulated among law officers, and it bore the likeness of one Henry Anson, wanted for murder. It had been issued by the sheriff at Virginia City, Nevada.

"There's writing at the bottom," Carla said.

Starbuck crossed to the window where the light was better and focused his eyes on the faint scrawl on the lower portion of the printed sheet.

Cancel previous request for information on man named Damon Friend. Has been cleared by confession of Dutch Ziegler. Friend located here in hospital dying from gunshot wounds.

Halverson, Sheriff

"Isn't Friend the name your brother goes

by?" Carla asked when Starbuck had finished reading.

A grim smile crossed Shawn's face. Ben was alive, hurt, but alive — at least that's how it was when the wanted dodger was sent to Bishop. He nodded in answer to her question.

"Reckon that explains why Griff Mulky said he didn't know what Arlie wanted to tell me. He had Ben's real name in mind."

"If your brother's wounded, and in a hospital, he could still be there — in Virginia City."

Starbuck laid the poster on a nearby table. "All depends on how long ago Arlie got this."

"I wish I could tell you. It could have been months. . . . I'm sorry, Shawn."

"Still something to go on — and if Ben's dead I want to know it," Starbuck said, picking up his hat. "Only one way to find out — go there."

Carla frowned, disappointment in her eyes. "Must you leave right away? I'd hoped I could somehow thank you for all you've done."

"No need," he said, moving to the door. "But like as not I'll see you again someday. . . . *Adios*."

"Goodbye, Shawn," Carla murmured.

We hope you have enjoyed this Large Print book. Other Thorndike Press or Chivers Press Large Print books are available at your library or directly from the publishers.

For more information about current and upcoming titles, please call or write, without obligation, to:

Thorndike Press
P.O. Box 159
Thorndike, Maine 04986 USA
Tel. (800) 257-5157

OR

Chivers Press Limited
Windsor Bridge Road
Bath BA2 3AX
England
Tel. (0225) 335336

All our Large Print titles are designed for easy reading, and all our books are made to last.